IN THE DEVIL'S POCKET

IN THE DEVIL'S POCKET

By

Michael T. Henry

Argus Enterprises International, Inc.

North Carolina****New Jersey

www.a-argusbooks.com

In The Devil's Pocket © *2009*
All rights reserved by: Michael T. Henry

A-Argus Better Book Publishers, LLC

For information:
A-Argus Better Book Publishers, LLC
Post Office Box 914
Kernersville, North Carolina 27285
www.a-argusbooks.com

ISBN: 978-0-9819075-2-9
ISBN: 0-9819075-2-0

Book Cover designed by Dubya

Printed in the United States of America

DEDICATION

TO ALL THE DREAMERS AND
BELIEVERS OF THE WORLD

CHAPTER ONE
JOHN BAYLEY

Generations ago, deep in the Appalachian Mountains, a shockwave was set in motion that will shake the world for generations to come. For millions of years, the Appalachians have spread their roots for hundreds of miles and provided a thriving habitat to all who tread across the forest floor. The mountains have always remained oblivious in the never-ending struggle between good and evil. Somewhere along the way, the line between good and evil has become blurred. The mountains were forced to join the struggle for life.

For the past few hundred years, modern man's overconfident intelligence and need to control the environment has amputated the mountains extremities to the heart. Eventually, indolence and prosperity began to prick at the Appalachian's soul. The mountains opened a portal through an expanding coal mine and released an evil hand that would touch countless lives. Man was evil's most dangerous weapon, and the lives molested by the hand molded one man's mind: John Bayley. Long before he was born, John was chosen to carry mankind's burden.

John is a young man now and trying to chisel his place in the world. He has no direction and his heart yearns to know his heritage. John can feel that he has a greater purpose, but he has no idea that his destiny began over sixty years ago and involves so many diverse strangers. His great-grandfather worked for a small coal mine in the heart of the Appalachian Mountains and lived with his family in the small town that sprung up close to the strip mine. The mine was thriving, and the town was booming as more and more people filtered out of the hollows for the opportunity of a more comfortable life.

John's great-grandfather was driving up the mountain on his way to work when a runaway coal truck rounded a curve and smashed head on into his car, killing him instantly. The mine's owner was an honest and kind man who vowed to financially support the family left behind. The mine expanded by the day and the owner became richer by the day. With success came temptation, and almost overnight the owner became addicted to women and booze. His afflictions consumed him as his money disappeared, and his business dealings suffered. Some say he was cursed by the mountain for raping her resources while others say that he just dug to close to Hell. The mine closed with the owner bankrupt and laying on his deathbed.

Ω

With the closing of the mine, the town quickly fell into poverty. First the businesses left town followed by the families one by one. John's family had nowhere to go and no one to help them and absolutely no money. They struggled every day just to feed themselves. Only a handful of families remained in town trying to hold onto what once was. The only thing to do was to survive and comfort each other. John's grandmother gave birth to his mother, Lucy, when she was fifteen. She desperately tried to raise Lucy but just couldn't care for her daughter. She would have died before she hurt Lucy, but her family and the rest of the town pressured her into abandoning Lucy.

Ω

Lucy was left on the doorstep of a small orphanage on the west side of the mountains. She was raised with strong Christian values, hard work, hard studies, and no material possessions what so ever. She flourished in the orphanage, despite her living conditions, and it was soon realized that she was quite intelligent. The temptation of a better life eventually lead Lucy to a nearby university to test for a scholarship. When the university discovered that she was a genius, they were eager to have her on campus and in their classrooms under a watchful eye. Soon the university decided they wanted Lucy on the payroll and provided her with anything she wanted, including a private residence.

Ω

Lucy was a young, beautiful, scientist working on the world's most complicated problems. Although her life was far better than she had ever dreamed growing up in the orphanage, she often confided to a friend that she felt her life was not her own. Then one day out of the blue, Lucy didn't show up for work. She was eventually found in her apartment, locked in the bathroom. When the police pried the door open, they found Lucy sitting on the floor hitting herself on the head with both hands and frantically screaming that there was something in her head. After a couple of painful weeks in the hospital, her official diagnosis was a nervous breakdown. Everybody figured that she just snapped from all the pressure that she was under and her radical lifestyle change. She was sent to a secluded insane asylum with the hope that a few weeks of rest and relaxation would snap her back to reality.

Ω

Lucy was enjoying her trip up and down through the old forest on her way to the asylum. She was escaping her agonizing pain by gazing deep into the woods that seemed to be beckoning her. Even though she was born in the mountains, she couldn't remember ever being in them. She could feel that, once her ordeal was over, she belonged in the rural landscape. Finally, Lucy arrived on top of a broad plateau covered with large boulders and towering pines speckled with massive, ancient oak trees. As the asylum began to appear through the trees, it was a beautiful but unnerving sight. The huge stone fortress demanded the respect of all who laid eyes on it. When Lucy passed through the front gate she was overcome with fear. She could feel evil all around her and wondered why there was the gate she had just come through. Lucy begged to be taken home and physically struggled against the orderlies as they dragged her through the door.

Ω

Once inside the asylum, Lucy quickly found herself restrained to a bed. She continually screamed that there was something in her head, while nurses injected mind-numbing drugs into her arm. Lucy cried out in pain and begged for someone to help her every day and could not understand why everybody just ignored her. Weeks turned into months and the university cut their losses and abandoned Lucy. Eventually, the powerful drugs had Lucy in such a comatose state that her restraints were removed. She was given her medication orally while she aimlessly roamed around like a zombie.

At the time, the asylum was on the cutting edge of technology in the mental health field. Looking back, their treatments more resembled barbaric torture. The medical staff was as competent as anywhere in the world, they were just unaware of how incompetent the human race still was. There was much more than met the eye at the asylum to those with an open mind. The asylum provided many beneficial jobs to the local area, but nobody ever lasted longer than a year. Urban legends whispered through the air for miles around that the asylum itself was a living monster that used the doctor's ignorance to feed its desire for human pain and suffering. Stories of torture, demonic possessions, and an evil spirit in the air as thick as fog was exactly what attracted a deeply disturbed young man to work at the asylum.

He was a Satanist who wore his beliefs on his skin and was hired as the nightshift janitor. He truly believed that he was a soldier in Satan's army. Everybody thought that he should have been a patient instead of an employee, but in the last ten years not one person ever lasted more than two nights doing his job.

Ω

Lucy was so out of it that she would sleep through the janitor strapping her arms and torso down to her bed but usually awoke when he was raping her in the middle of the night while the security guards were too afraid to leave the front desk. After a couple months of nightly visits from the Satanist janitor, it was discovered that Lucy was pregnant. Somehow she had enough state of mind to know what was happening to her and to know that she did not want her baby exposed to her medication. She began slipping her pills through the holes in the adjustable legs on the desk in her room every chance she could. Lucy somehow suppressed the pain and escaped to a far-away place in her own mind for the rest of her pregnancy.

Ω

After a long agonizing pregnancy, Lucy finally went into labor. The last thing she remembered was a big needle going into her arm. When she regained consciousness, she was in her room alone, as usual. For a moment she felt at peace while she tried to get her wits about her. She felt pain in her stomach. In an instant all the terror flooded back into her mind as she frantically pulled up her gown and seen the stitches where they cut her baby from her womb. She screamed for the nurse, demanding to see her baby.

As the orderlies rushed in and strapped her to the bed, the nurse assured Lucy that she did not have a baby and stuck her with another needle. At that moment, Lucy lost all hope of ever seeing her baby or getting out of the hospital.

Ω

Lucy knew that if she kept fighting with the hospital staff she had no control over anything in her life. She decided to cooperate and act as if nothing was wrong. Keeping quiet was extremely difficult for Lucy with the excruciating pain in her head and the gut wrenching heartache of having her baby stolen. Eventually the staff removed her restraints and started giving her medication orally again. Now she had control of at least one thing. Unable to take any-more, Lucy crawled out of bed, pulled apart the legs of her desk and took all the medication that she had hidden for nine months.

Ω

Lucy lay on the autopsy table, and the doctor that had been treating her during the past year was eager to cut open her skull and study her brain. As they pried the top of her skull off, they found a small bloody hemorrhage. When they started examining it, with hopes of making an exciting new medical discovery, it moved. As the two doctors realized that it was some sort of leach-like parasite, they were overcome by an uneasy feeling that sent cold chills down their spines. The two doctors panicked and quickly shoved her body into the incinerator. As her body was cremated, the autopsy report was marked as inconclusive. The two agreed never to talk about what they found to anybody. Lucy really did have something in her head, and she could have been cured with a simple surgery. Her doctor struggled with his conscience for a couple weeks until everyone had forgotten all about Lucy. The only thing left from her whole life was in a thin file in the basement of a mental hospital.

Ω

John was born a healthy, happy, baby boy, and it wasn't long until a loving couple that couldn't conceive a child of their own adopted him. The hospital administration was quite proud of themselves for turning such a tragedy into a triple win situation. John had a bright future with his new parents, and the administrators made a little money by providing the loving parents with a baby that had no past. John's life was good for a few months until one day John went into respiratory arrest. By the time the ambulance arrived, his mother had revived him. He was taken to a hospital for testing, but nothing seemed to be wrong with him. He was sent home. Things were good for a couple of weeks, and then it happened again with the same results. After about a half dozen times, suspicions began to arise. While interrogating the mother a doctor decided to hold John for observation and notified the authorities of his suspicions.

Ω

Investigators set up a hidden security camera in John's room, and after the next attack they reviewed the tape. As they watched in disbelief, there was John's adoptive mother holding the palm of her hand firmly over his mouth and pinching off his nose with her index finger and thumb. She held him relentlessly until his little arms and legs stopped kicking and thrashing, and then she frantically called for help. Most believe the woman became accustomed to receiving attention and pity from friends and family while unsuccessfully trying to conceive a child for years. Shortly after she adopted John, the attention stopped. She became like a drug addict needing their fix. John had no apparent brain damage from oxygen deprivation, but there seemed to be some minor lung damage that made him easily winded.

Ω

In as much as John had legal parents, he was placed in the foster care system. Everybody felt sorry for him, so he was placed with the best family in the system. The family was devout Christians that never missed church on Sunday and had trouble making ends meet from taking care of unwanted children. They took John in and treated him as one of their own. When they noticed a problem with his legs they immediately sought medical attention. When he crawled it was more like dragging a set of gnarled up legs behind him. When he was at the age that he should have been walking, he couldn't even straighten his legs out to stand. It was as if his muscles and tendons were permanently contracted. Painful physical therapy was started.

Ω

Taking care of a handicapped child meant bigger
checks to offset the extra cost and work. When it became apparent that John would be in a wheelchair the
rest of his life, there was money to make the house
handicap accessible. There was even money for a
new van, which the family desperately needed. Everybody admired the devotion it took to selflessly raise
somebody else's special-needs child. They went to
church every Sunday and praised God for what they
had and prayed for John. They even scraped up
enough money to tithe every week. The whole community was so inspired that they regularly took up
special offerings in church for the family. There was
even a half-dozen or so donation jars on the counters
of convenience stores and gas stations around the
area.

Ω

One day, on a scheduled visit, John's caseworker
showed up with a young trainee fresh out of college.
The visit was a required checkup, and everything was
up to par as usual. They discussed a medical bill that
the state was questioning whether or not it was
John's, and the caseworker assured the mother she
would take care of it. John's extensive therapy schedule left little free time, so the caseworkers were
soon on their way. On the car ride to the next stop,
the slightly over-zealous trainee—ready to fix the
world's problems— mentioned that for the thousands
of dollars the family received he did not see much,

other than a couple of chintzy plywood ramps and a wheelchair lift in the van. He was quickly scolded and told that they were the best foster family in the system and not to be giving them any trouble. Then he was told that he had far bigger problems he needed to worry about, and the subject was dropped.

Ω

Eventually, the young caseworker's training was over. He was officially a state-certified foster care employee and out on his own. One hot summer day, he saw John's foster mother walking into a beauty salon alone. He figured it would be a good time for a spot inspection, or at least he could snoop around. On the ride to the house, he knew he would get an ass-chewing for what he was about to do. He did not care though, and he was passionate about doing the job he was getting paid to do. Frankly, he was sick and tired of being treated like he was stupid and everyone just shaking their head and walking away from him every time he opened his mouth. He had respect for his elders, but the way he saw it was, why should he have to follow their example when they had everything screwed up? If his generation was going to carry the burden of a future for younger generations because of years of older generations plundering resources and money, he was going to do what he wanted to do.

Ω

When he got to the house, the teenage daughter answered the door. He identified himself and asked for the mother. The girl informed him that she was babysitting while her mother was running errands, and he would have to come back another time. He could tell the girl was nervous, so he threatened to call the police and have them escort him in. She then reluctantly left him in. As he looked around, everything looked normal. He started doubting himself. When he asked to see John, he was told that John was sleeping and could not be disturbed. He informed the girl that he could not leave until he saw John and to just show him where John's room was. The girl had a look on her face like a murderer about to confess as she took him downstairs and showed him John's door. The caseworker opened the door. There was John with his ankles strapped to his upper thighs with ratchet straps and another pair of ratchet straps pulling his knees towards the floor, painfully spreading his legs apart.

Ω

The caseworker stood there in total shock, not knowing what to do. At first, he thought it was part of John's therapy, but then he realized that was why John was in therapy. As he phoned for help and released the straps, the situation became clear to him. He wondered what kind of monsters these people were, to abuse a kid like that day after day just to scam the state out of more money. The girl sat in the corner looking like she was relieved that it was all over. The caseworker looked at her and thought about how he had saved a child that day, only to probably have her and her siblings to take care of the next day.

Ω

The caseworker was traumatized by his discovery that day, so he decided to take a few days off. One morning he read an article about what had happened in the local newspaper. The only thing the foster mother had to say for justification was that they gave some of the money to the church. As he read on in disgust, there was a quote from the family's pastor proclaiming that the church had forgiven them of their sins. The caseworker thought that the ironic thing was that everybody thought they were the greatest people in town. Then he wondered how many wolves in sheep's clothing there were in the world. He learned a valuable lesson that he carried throughout his life, which was not to trust anyone who makes an effort to show you how good they are. He gathered his composure and returned to work that afternoon ready to save children from these evil people.

Ω

John was placed in another home and continued on with his painful therapy. This time, he was making progress. Everybody involved was quite thrilled to be steadily moving forward, instead of one step forward one day and two steps back the next morning. John cried out in pain almost every day throughout the ordeal as his therapists relentlessly pushed him to progress towards a normal life. It took months and months of excruciating therapy, and eventually John was walking and started school. His hips and knees never fully recovered, but it was only noticeable when he ran. John's new home was far from perfect, but it was a great deal better than the first five years of his life. If there was any good that came from John's ordeal, it was that the foster kids were under a more watchful eye and the foster parents under even more scrutiny.

Ω

All in all, John was a pretty normal happy kid who excelled scholastically in school. His only problem at that time was kids making fun of him in gym class. Children can be relentlessly cruel, and many thought John should not be subjected to the cruelty of gym class. His doctors were afraid of a sedentary lifestyle that would regress his physical therapy, so John was made to participate in physical education. Throughout the years he learned to suppress his emotions. Crying or showing anger only made things worse and drew more attention to himself. Eventually John had pretty much become a recluse. He often fantasized that someday doctors would have the technology to fix his damaged joints and lungs, and he would have them make him faster and stronger than anyone.

Ω

There was a tall, lanky, irritating kid named Nick in their class who was the one usually making fun of John. The boy was taller, stronger and a better athlete than all the other kids his age but was a little insecure about his intelligence. Any chance to draw attention to somebody else's shortcomings was a chance to hide his. Then one day Nick was making fun of John, in gym class, and an awkward redheaded girl named Amy began defending John. Nick really began taunting him then, calling him a sissy who had to have a girl fight his battles. John usually only had to contain himself for a short time until it was all over, but with Nick's new ammunition, it just kept coming and coming. John gritted his teeth as he tried to absorb the abuse, but there was too much. He erupted like a volcano. With a growl-like scream, John launched a basketball from his chest so hard that it hit Nick square in the face and bounced back over John's head. Nick staggered but did not go down. John's anger started to turn to fear. John watched Nick and realized that the lights were on, but nobody was home. He quickly charged Nick, driving his fist into Nick's teeth. That one put Nick out cold and flat on his back. Everybody stared at John in disbelief like he was some kind of monster, except Amy who gave him a little smile as she turned away.

Ω

John soon found himself sitting in the school office while an intense debate raged on in the adjacent room. Nick dramatically moaned while he lay across the hall in the nurse's office with ice piled on top of his face. School administration, John's foster par-ents, and his caseworker were discussing him as if he was a budding serial killer. John could not under-stand why everyone was angry with him. He could not see why it was all right for Nick to make fun of him for years but not all right for him to defend him-

self. It seemed like every person had a rank in society, and the system would not let you better yourself.
The only person who supported John was Amy.
Even though he was mad at her for making things
worse, John could not help but to feel some appreciation for her trying to help him. Eventually he
thanked her, and a beautiful friendship began.

Ω

For weeks to come, the whole school talked about
what had happened. John was used to being the topic
of conversation but never about something other than
his disability. The kids were at the point in their lives
where everyone was separating into their cliques and
being labeled. For John, being a bad boy was far better than being a brainy handicapped kid. John started
getting into trouble just to keep attention off his legs.
It got to the point where he would sit around and
think of things he could do to get into trouble. He
purposely left his grades fall because, of course, at
that age it was un-cool to be smart. The older John
got and the more trouble he got into, the less patience
his foster families had with him. Being shuffled from
one place to another taught John a lot about human
nature. Soon he could read people like a book. He
developed a unique talent for manipulating them into
doing what he wanted without them realizing that it
was not what they wanted. By the time he was a
young teenager, John became so good that he could
bullshit his way out of just about any trouble he got
in to. He could get caught shoplifting and have a job
in the same store before the police showed up.

Ω

Over the years, Amy had blossomed from an awkward young girl into a beautiful, shapely, young woman. Puberty had hit John like a freight train, and he fell head-over-heels in love with her. He thought about her every conscious moment of his life but was too afraid to tell her. Every time they were together, John felt as if he was having an anxiety attack and was afraid he was going to vomit. Anytime another boy would show interest in Amy, John would panic and ask himself why he didn't tell her. Finally, after a couple of years of torture, John confessed his love to Amy. She busted up laughing. After she realized that he was dead serious, she told him that they had been friends for a long time, and she did not think of him in that way. Amy did not mean to be hurtful to John, but she ripped his heart right out of his chest.

Ω

John was devastated and embarrassed beyond all belief, so he really began to find trouble just to cope with his heartache. He even started picking fights, which took the bad-boy image a little too far. Nobody wanted to be around him. John would only pick fights with the ones that he knew would not fight or could not fight, which only made John look like an even bigger ass. John still harbored hope for him and Amy. Although she came from the lower social standing, she was never going back. She was in with the popular crowd now and would barely even associate with her old friends. John had heard that Amy was dating some jock. When he found out it was the irritating kid Nick that started their friendship, John became overwhelmed with feelings of betrayal. At that point, hating Nick was the only thing that he and Amy had in common. With that gone, John's hope began to diminish.

Ω

After several weeks of moping around, John decided to get hold of himself. The harsh reality of life had set in, and he knew that there was nothing he could do about it. He made himself stop fantasizing about Amy and concentrate on his life and the direction in which it was heading. He refocused on his childhood dreams of making himself better than all those who had ever disrespected him. John knew that the first thing he needed was money. The only attribute he had was his mind and his gift of persuasion. John realized that they were the only tools he had to work with to reach his desires. His grades skyrocketed once he applied himself, and he even got a part-time job cleaning up at a local department store. It was not long until the store's salespeople were splitting their commissions with John for every sale that he sent their way. John could sell anything to anyone.

Ω

Things were going good for John. He was focused and would not let anything distract him. Then one night, an opportunity presented itself on his way home from work. He came upon an idling car sitting along the road with its lights on. As he pulled in be-hind, he recognized the car as Nick's. John got out of his car to approach Nick but hesitated. He was not sure he wanted to see what was probably going on inside. He swallowed the lump in his throat as he approached the other car. He noticed a strong stench of alcohol. John looked in the car, and there was Nick slumped over the steering wheel, drunk. The car was sitting on a slight grade about two hundred feet from a sharp turn with a wooded embankment down over the side. Somehow, Nick managed to stop his car and put it into park before passing out and smashing into the trees. John jealously wondered how one person could be so lucky. This guy was everything John wanted to be, and when he was about to screw up, he somehow avoided it. Overcome by jealously, John reached in and jerked Nick's car into drive. As the car began to roll, John jumped in his car to follow. John envisioned Nick hitting a tree along the road, smashing up his car, and maybe getting a broken nose. John then planned to call the police to report an accident so Nick would get busted for drinking and driving.

As John followed Nick's car rolling along very slowly, he thought about nudging it along a little faster, but he decided against it. That would probably leave evidence on the cars that John was involved in the accident. Even if there were not much damage to Nick's car, he would still get busted for under-age drinking. When Nick's car finally reached the turn it somehow managed to miss every single tree for about three hundred feet while it accelerated down the bank to a tremendous speed. When the car finally hit a huge oak tree, it sounded like someone shot off a cannon. John sat there dumbfounded as he realized that his harmless manipulation had just turned into a serious assault. John started to get out of his car to help Nick until he thought about what would happen to him for his involvement. He panicked and sped off for home knowing full well that he could never talk about the incident to anyone and definitely could not report the accident.

Ω

Over the next couple of days, John had become quite paranoid while waiting to hear some news about the accident. John was too afraid to inquire about the accident, in case someone would wonder how he knew about it. He began to think that maybe nobody has found him yet, and that Nick could even be dead by now. As paranoia took over John's mind, he started doubting his memory of whether or not anyone else was there who may have seen him. He was terrified that he may have left evidence that could potentially connect him to the accident. John could not concentrate on anything and constantly tried to remember the exact details of the incident. Bits and pieces of visions kept popping into his head about people being there, or his tire tracks in the mud. He could not tell what was real, or what was paranoia. The more paranoid John became, the more he wished that he could take back his decision to screw with Nick's life. John was starting to think that maybe his life was going to be the one ruined from his actions.

Finally, John had heard that Nick was in the hospital recovering from surgery. He was going to be all right, other than a permanently scarred face and enough pins and screws in his bones to probably cause him to hobble around for the rest of his life.

Nobody, not even Nick, suspected anything other than just another teenager ruining their life over partying. John's paranoia subsided, but he could not help feeling guilty. Eventually, he convinced himself that it was not his fault. All he did was put the car in gear, and he did not have any control of where the car went. Furthermore, Nick put himself into that situation.

Ω

It was a rough couple of weeks for John's conscience, but when he heard that Amy broke it off with Nick, it was all worth it. Everything that John had been worrying and obsessing about ever since Nick and Amy got together, completely disappeared from his mind in an instant. This was his chance to make amends with Amy. John quickly maneuvered himself to casually run into her where they would be alone. He told her that he was sorry for what had happened to Nick, and he was there for her if she needed him. They talked awhile, and John walked away feeling better than he had in a long time. John and Amy's friendship was revived. They continued to laugh and carry on every time they saw each other. After a couple of months had gone by, John was sure that Amy was falling for him. He was so confident about it, he planned to kiss her the next time they were alone.

Ω

When the time had come for John to make his move on Amy, he was so nervous that he almost ran away.

He managed to gain control of himself, and he sat down beside her. They started one of their usual conversations. Within seconds John did not even know what the conversation was about and did not care. He was just trying to set up that first kiss, which was the only thing in the whole world that John really wanted. It was like running a gauntlet. John would wait for the right time to make his move, hesitate, and then realize that he had missed his chance. He became more and more frenzied until he decided that the next time she stopped talking, he was going for it. He was concentrating so hard that he almost missed what she had just told him. John hesitated one more time and asked Amy to repeat herself. She informed him that she had been seeing someone.

John just sat there completely speechless until Amy asked if he was all right. He wanted to scream, but he acted like it was no big deal. In a crackling voice, he asked her who it was. Amy excitedly told John about how cool her new boyfriend was, and how nice his car was. He even had his own place. With a puzzled look on his face, John asked the age of Amy's new boyfriend. She told him that he was twenty-seven. John had never even come close to experiencing what he was feeling at that moment, and something inside of him snapped. John exploded into a fit of rage, yelling at Amy about how the guy was a loser that couldn't get anyone his own age. He told her that her boyfriend was a predator that preyed on young girls because they were naive. Then John forcefully asked her if she was trying to screw with his head. Amy was scared and told John that she never wanted to talk to him again and to stay away from her. As she quickly walked away, John warned

Amy that her new boyfriend would probably try to get her pregnant as soon as she was of legal age, before she matured enough to see the truth.

Ω

At that point, John was so fed up with the stress that Amy caused him that he decided that he did not want anything to do with her anyhow. Accepting the fact that he would never be with Amy was easier than dealing with the constant appearance and disappearance of hope. John just needed to put Amy behind him and concentrate on his future. His life was so close to being his own that he could taste it. John desperately wanted to make something great out of his life, and he needed to concentrate on a career. John had no ties to anyone or anything. His future was wide open. He researched almost every job in the world and ranked them by pay and any attributes that he already had to perform them.

Ω

John's current foster dad was a quiet, honest man that barely even spoke to John, but when he saw John trying to choose a career, he offered his advice. John thought that his foster dad was stupid and oblivious to everything around him, but all in all he was a pretty decent foster parent so John figured that he would indulge the guy. After a short conversation, John realized that for the first time he was wrong about someone. Turns out John's foster dad was a fairly intelligent guy and knew exactly what was going on. Instead of running his mouth all the time like a lot of people, he was listening to everything and taking it all in. He warned John about some of the unforeseen surprises in life. He also told John his theory that the government kept the workingman from getting ahead, which enabled the country to survive. The middle-class working man had to support society on both sides of him. The only reason the upper-class let the lower-class receive support was to keep the average Joe's mind off of paying the upper-class dearly to run his life. He then told John not to believe a word he or anybody else tells him, but to put it in the back of his mind, think about it, and make his own decision later. As John's foster dad was leaving the room he said, "The truth will be what you believe it is."

Ω

Over the next couple of weeks, John continued re-searching careers and pondering whether or not there was any truth in his foster dad's sermon. Then, late one night right before bed, John's foster dad asked him if he had made a decision yet. John had a pretty good idea of what he wanted to do but was reluctant to say. John's foster dad said, "You would be a great salesman. As good as you can bullshit people, you could sell a man his own house. Hell, maybe you should be an insurance salesman."

John just chuckled and shook his head. John thought a little while and then told his foster dad that he was thinking about going to seminary school. John could tell by the puzzled look on his foster dad's face that he was confused and wondering how John had become so religious. John told him that he would basically be a salesman. John said, "Redemption is for sale and people are buying as much as they can."

John's foster dad cracked a terrified little smile and said, "God save the world from you."

The comment triggered a fantasy flash of having the world's respect, and John realized an unforeseen opportunity presented by his career choice.

CHAPTER TWO
INDEPENDENCE

PRESENT

John soon finds himself at a small church in a depressed little town nestled along the west side of the Appalachians. He has been cast out into the world, all alone and nowhere to hide. Ready or not, he must forge his own path through life. John stands before a handful of devout families in a very awkward situation. His congregation welcomes him with open arms, but not open hearts. John can tell that they are just going through the motions that they are accustomed to. John knows what he must do. He was born to preach, it is in his blood. Within weeks, John revives life into a town that has lost sight of their own identity for decades.

Ω

Even though John knows his decision to become a preacher was more of a career choice than a calling, he begins to believe that he was chosen to lead his people. He even admits to his congregation of how he chose to become a preacher and just chalks it up to God working in mysterious ways. John soon realizes that if he stands before his congregation and confesses his sins, they love him even more. Sometimes he even makes things up, especially when counseling someone on a personal level, just to make them feel better about themselves. The better John makes people feel about themselves the more they want to listen to him, which keeps the pews full every Sunday. John figures that it's all right with God for him to play people in order to keep them in church and to bring new people in. John has his congregation so buffaloed that they do not think about what they are doing all week long. Just as long as they come to church, pray and tithe—especially tithe—they are saved.

Ω

The church is nearly filled to capacity and the collection plates are overflowing every Sunday. John's church is part of an organized denomination of churches and governed by a council, which is very pleased with him. John is proud to be the organization's number one minister but can't help to feel a little jealous about the council reaping the monetary benefits of his hard work. The church was struggling to make ends meet when John became the preacher, and within months the membership has doubled and the offerings have almost tripled. John knows there is plenty of money left over after the church's operating expenses are paid. He becomes very frustrated when he requests money, to improve his living conditions or for church activities, and is denied.

John decides to start an activity fund where, unbeknownst to the council, a small percentage of the collection will be taken and put in an account in his name. The fund is for soup kitchens, toys for poor children at Christmas and social activities and such. He prints weekly reports on the account balance and encourages his congregation to suggest ways to use the money. Everybody is grateful that John is putting some of their hard-earned money back into the community. Only John and the church treasurer count and divide up the collection money. The long-time treasurer, who can hide her own Easter eggs, keeps her records in John's small office in the church all week long. It's easy for John to alter the activity slush fund and transfer the leftover money into a separate personal account. The treasurer can barely remember her name from week to week, let alone account deposits, and nobody suspects a thing. John's whole life is his church, so the skimmed money is still in the church. He is just preparing for a rainy day that his people might be in need, or at least that is how he justifies what he is doing.

Ω

For the moment, John is satisfied with his life. There is always plenty of money in his pocket, and he has become an important person in the community. Even people who do not attend his church know who he is and treats him with respect, which is something that John has yearned for throughout his life. John is a man, though, and there is one thing that keeps distracting him more and more: women. There are plenty of young Christian women for John to date, but none of them satisfy his physical desires. When it comes to emotions, he discovers that he is still in love with Amy. The problem progressively gets worse.

He starts fantasizing about women sitting before him while he is giving sermons. It's like hitting puberty for the second time, and he is constantly having fantasies about practically every woman that he knows. It even gets to the point where he is not accomplishing anything all day long because he is too busy daydreaming. John decides that he has to do something about his problem when he almost makes a mistake with a teenage girl on a youth group outing.

Ω

John figures the best thing to stop his new obsession is to satisfy it. John does not want to make a commitment to any of the single women in his congregation, and he knows that he can't have one-night stands with them. He begins driving to the nearest city and hiring prostitutes. With no strings attached and nobody aware of what he is doing, it is the perfect solution to his problem and he can concentrate on his job. A visit to the city every few weeks quickly turns into weekly trips. His obsession is turning into an addiction. He is not satisfying anything, and he's wanting more and more. Eventually, he is hiring two or three women for a couple of days and sneaking them home to the parsonage. John's skimmed money is disappearing fast, so he wants to make sure he gets his money's worth. He is losing control of himself and nothing will satisfy him. It's not long until John and his entourage start role-playing inside the church. Another local minister, who hates John for taking half of his congregation, is watching like a hawk, waiting for some dirt on John. When the minister sees John sneaking the women into the church, he calls a tabloid paper. The minister and a photographer team up and wait for the next week's fun. John is practically broke and almost dodges the bullet, but he manages to scrape enough money together for another romp. The photographer makes his career when he sneaks into the church and takes some of the most shocking pictures ever.

Ω

After it's all over, the other minister can't contain himself and confronts John. He tells John everything and even shows some of his own pictures. John wants to strangle his scrawny little neck but is overcome with panic. John storms inside his house and starts to frantically pace back and forth trying to think of an excuse for his actions. There is no excuse. He does not even know how he is going to look his congregation in the eye. John can feel the respect that he has gained slipping away. He can't face his peers. As he packs his bags to leave town before the news gets out, he wonders how he is going to support himself. He wasted all of his banked money on prostitutes and has no one to help him. He will have to get a job just to put a meager roof over his head and food into his stomach. All he can think about is that he's losing everything he has built up from nothing. The church is John's church. It drives him crazy that people are interfering in his business and that someone else will step right into his shoes. He calms himself down and decides that he is going to fight for what is rightfully his. John thinks that maybe if he confesses before he is busted, he might just get away with it.

Ω

Sunday morning John appears before a packed church and begins frantically sobbing as he confesses about the prostitutes. John falls to his knees, throws his hands into the air, and begs for forgiveness. It only takes a couple of minutes of John's passionate performance until his congregation is running to him, hugging him, and telling him that they love him and they forgive him. With tears in his eyes, John manipulates his congregation into revering him even more than they have before. John has his followers wrapped around his little finger, but the church council will not be so forgiving. When the news finally gets out, the council rolls into town like a swat team. They chew John up one side and down the other and threaten to excommunicate him from the church right there on the spot. John is getting angry, but he knows to keep his mouth shut. He only tells them that the whole congregation has already forgiven him, and that he will use it to bring in more people. He knows the council is more concerned with income than virtuousness. The council decides to give him another chance. Before they leave, one council member asks John, in an insinuating way, how he afforded to pay the prostitutes. John just cracks a little smile and says, "The girls gave the church a ten percent discount." Nobody else thinks it is funny and, as they leave, they warn John that they are watching him.

Ω

John has been put up on a pedestal so much that he can hardly stand to be put under anybody's thumb. He is angry with the council, but at the same time relieved with the outcome of his scandal. John wants some vengeance. His fellow minister that ratted him out becomes his new obsession. John will make the minister pay dearly for interfering with his comfortable lifestyle. The other church still has some influential members of the community, and John makes it his mission to acquire them. John picks out one person at a time and works on getting them into his church. He actually profiles each person and their family. He always finds a link between him and who he is working on, usually a third party, to try and convince the people to come to his church. John even puts himself in the right place at the right time to casually run into his target and start a friendly conversation. One by one, all of the important people in the area are showing up to listen to John on Sunday.

Ω

John hates not being in total control of everything. At least twice a week, he obsesses to the point of rage about the council threatening him. He knows that if his congregation grows large enough and he brings in enough money, he has a chance to control the church council. John puts more and more into his sermons every week. His sermons become more about praising his congregation and telling them that they are on the path to everlasting life because they are following him, rather than living their lives up to God's expectations. John interprets everything that he reads out of the Bible into whatever best suites him and his congregation. He makes it as easy as possible to be saved, and that is what most of his people want.

John even takes to advertising. He leases a couple of billboards around the area and even makes a commercial on a local radio station. His biggest advertising campaigns are thinking up of charitable events and making sure the local weekly newspaper is there to cover them. John pulls off every stunt and fundraiser he can think of. He even starts a health clinic at the church once a month for people who can't afford decent health care. John gets doctors and nurses to donate their time. He even talks a pharmaceutical company into donating basic medication for the publicity of helping the poor rural Americans. Being a small town, there are not many destitute people. John drives to the city and hires homeless individuals to visit the clinic and find a reporter to tell about how John is saving their life.

John's tactics are working well. John's publicity stunts are pumping his image to the level of sainthood, and his followers have never been happier in their lives. It seems the council members are blinded by the money that is coming in, and they have forgotten all about John and his prostitutes. John's rival minister has to close the doors on his church because John has taken almost every member out of his congregation. The minister has to leave town. As he is leaving, John approaches him and says, "I have forgiven you, but evidently God has not." The minister just jumps in his vehicle and heads off for the next small town that needs a preacher. John is very focused when he is working towards a goal, but once he reaches that goal he becomes distracted again.

Ω

It's a hot summer day and John's youth group is holding a car wash to raise money for a summer church camp. One of John's loyal followers notices John starring at his young wife in her tight shorts and tank top all afternoon. John watches every single glistening bead of sweat and water trickle down across the young woman's body. He intensely fantasizes about taking her into his arms and laying her down across the hood of the soaking wet car. John looks like a bird dog pointing out a pheasant. He has no idea that he is being that obvious, so he suspects nothing when the man invites him for supper next week. John arrives on time and eats a delicious meal. Since the couple have no children, John is prepared for a few hours of socializing before going home. The man explains to John how important he is to the community, and that everybody is grateful for what he has done. The man goes on to say that the congregation realizes just how much John has helped them. They want to help John in return. He tells John about how the council has removed their beloved ministers before, and that they are going to do whatever it takes to keep John. The man stands up and tells John to please take his wife as he walks out the door.

Ω

John just sits there dumbfounded, not realizing exactly what the man is getting at, until his wife stands in front of him and begins undressing. John jumps up stuttering and fumbling around as he tries to resist the woman. He is caught off guard and embarrassed. He tries to drape the woman's clothes across her body, while he is taking a good peek. She grabs John and tells him, "What happens here stays here, and it's nobody else's business. This way you won't be going out and getting into trouble, giving the council a reason to remove you." John figures that he can get away with just about anything with the council by now, but he decides to keep that thought private. He not so reluctantly gives in to temptation.

Ω

John has just had the best experience of his life. It was even better than roll-playing with the prostitutes inside the church. John relives the evening in his head over and over for the rest of the week. When Sunday rolls around, he can't look the husband in the eye and can't take his eyes off of the wife. He thinks it was a once-in-a-lifetime opportunity. When another couple invites him to diner the next week, John expects nothing but another good meal. When it happens again, John is very excited to see a pattern emerging. Turns out there are four of John's male followers that are willing to share their wives to keep him out of trouble. Some of the wives are easier on the eyes than others, but John is more than willing to oblige all of them. He tells each one of them that God will reward them for their sacrifices made for the good of the church.

Ω

John can't imagine his life getting any better. After a month of Sundays with standing room only, John has one of his members take pictures of all the people. He takes the pictures to the church council to petition for the building of a bigger church. John even sketches out some plans of his ideas, including his quite comfortable living quarters inside the building. John pitches the point that he can't bring in more people if they can't fit in the door. Also, it would be cheaper to maintain one building rather than a church and a parsonage. There is a brief discussion, and the council tells John that they need some time to think about it and they will get back to him with their decision. On the way home, John feels good about the meeting. He is confident that the council will approve his ideas. It makes perfect sense, and it is just good business.

Ω

After a few weeks the council schedules a meeting with John. This time they are coming to John, and he takes that as a good sign. He has even picked out a large building lot in town, and he figures the council is coming to look at it. At the meeting, the council informs John that his request is denied. John just stands there with a blank expression on his face. They explain that all of John's points are valid, but all of the buildings have long since been paid for. It would take years to gain back the cost of building a new extravagant church. They just can't justify it. The council informs John that they do have a solution for him to bring more people in. They take John to the second church that he will be preaching at every Sunday.

The other church is in a small town about twenty miles away. John will have to perform Sunday services in the other church earlier in the morning, and then drive like a maniac to preach at his original church before lunch. John is furious and can hardly contain himself, being trapped in a vehicle for the half-hour trip. Once at the new church, they meet with some of the faithful members and go over all the details. It doesn't take long for John to realize that it will be like starting all over again, nursing a struggling church back to life. John is in a power struggle with the council, and he just had the wind knocked out of his sails. On the way home, he keeps thinking about how every time he thinks he has control of the council, they show him exactly who is in charge. John is good and sick of it and starting to get discouraged. He decides that he will no longer bust his ass for somebody else's benefit. When they return home, one of the council members tells John that when he fills both churches to capacity, they will then build him a new church right in the middle of the two towns. John wants to knock the smart-ass smirk right off the guys face, but just turns and walks away.

Ω

John is furious at the council, but at the same time humbled by the council's authority. John is becoming extremely confident in himself. When the council knocks him down a peg or two, he can't help but to become a little depressed. The first couple of Sundays at the new church, John pretty much just goes through the motions. After a while, John's pride gets the better of him, and he begins to turn on his charm. He soon makes some new friends and sees some new opportunities. John tries to see the bright side of his new situation. He figures that as good as things were for him before, now they can be doubled. Still, John would rather go without something that he can have, than to give the council anything extra.

Ω

Alongside the highway that passes through a gap in the mountains between the two churches sits a warehouse that is for sale or lease. The warehouse is in the middle of a beautiful little valley that vanishes up into the mountains. The only other access to the valley is by an abandoned dirt road that snaked for miles through the mountain towering above the valley. Few people ever brave the treacherous path, and it is not marked on a modern map. As John drives by the place two times a Sunday, he is usually too busy stewing over the council to think anything about it. Then one Sunday while he is driving by, John looks over at the place and thinks about how it would be a good building for the council to consider renovating into a new church. Then it hits John like a bolt of lightning from the sky. He can go out on his own and start an independent church. If he can come up with enough money to secure a large building and remodel it into a church and living quarters, he is sure that most of his congregation will follow him. Then there will be no one to answer to, or nobody to control the money John works so hard for. John immediately starts working out the details and comes up with a vengeful plan. If the council wants him to fill both churches he will. Then he will take it all away from them. John wants to make sure they know exactly what they lose by crossing him.

Ω

John meets with the owner to investigate the property. It doesn't take John long to decide that it will be the perfect place for him to start his own church. With a few walls, windows, and doors, the warehouse can be made into a nice church. There is ten acres of ground around the building so there will be an ample area for parking and outside activities. More importantly, there is a little more privacy. John is in a financial position to start leasing right away but has experienced enough to know that if he is going to do this, he wants to flat out own the property. John wants to be solely in control of everything and does not want to answer to anyone. He doesn't even want a bank holding the mortgage. John manages to sweet talk the owner into a deal were he will lease, just to hold the place until he raises enough money to buy, with a percentage of the rent going towards the purchase price.

Ω

Once John has his building secured, he sets to work raising the money and securing his congregation. He divides his time between nurturing his second church to grow, just like he did with the first one, and getting support from his established followers for the move.

John starts talking to his original congregation one by one or in small groups. He figures that if he is already at the point where some of them will share their wives with him, they will follow him anywhere. John is taking no chances though. He knows that he will have to be patient and well prepared. Secrecy will be of the utmost importance. John can't have his income come under any scrutiny from the council. He wants to be the one to drop the bombshell on the council. He makes a list of the whole congregation in order of importance, either by social standing or financial ability. John writes and memorizes a speech and goes right down his list delivering his sales pitch.

Ω

John's speech is about the sin and corruption in a unionized church. He tells his followers that God does not intend church to be a business. Church is a gathering of people to worship God. How they worship and what is done with the people's offerings is nobody's business but God's and the people. Just about everyone that John talks to commits to becoming a member of his new independent church. John is confident that the ones who do not will soon follow. He asks all of his people for more contributions to go directly into the slush fund while he slowly takes more and more out of the offering. John is careful not to make any sudden changes to arouse suspicion with the council. John also asks his people to think of and coordinate fundraisers to lessen the burden on his time.

Ω

John's people really step up to help make his dream happen. There are many large contributions right away, followed by a fundraiser of some sort almost every week. Meanwhile, John is working overtime charming his new congregation. The new churches congregation is growing even faster than the first one. John is trying to be patient, but he decides to push things a little and informs his second congregation of his plans. John sets up two collections every Sunday. One is for John's proposed church and the other goes to the union church. The people can put their money where they want. John knows that not pressuring people and acting like he is giving them an opportunity is the fastest way to get their support. John's plan is working perfectly, and his second slush fund is growing as fast as the congregation.

Ω

Some of John's original followers express concerns about joining with the other church. John tells them that they need the people from the other church to get started and they can weed out the congregation later. John knows he is flat out lying to them. He will never turn anyone away as long as they have cash or a check in their pocket on Sunday. John even loses some followers simply because church is getting too big for them. It doesn't matter though, because John has the most important people right in his pocket. He will even go out of his way to do things for certain people, just so they feel like they owe him. John also knows that the more he can do and give to other people, the more he can get away with.

Ω

John is growing increasingly nervous by the day, fearing the council will find out what he has been up too. His funds are growing by the thousands every week, but that isn't fast enough. John comes up with his own fundraiser to take advantage of the money he is spending to lease his property. He organizes a religious festival. It is an all day Saturday event. John lines up live music for all day, everything from gospel groups to Christian rock bands, and charges a cover charge to get on the grounds. Many of John's followers provide all kinds of food and drinks for sale. Some people make donations of arts and crafts to be sold. Advertisement flyers are sent out and newspaper ads taken out for about a fifty-mile radius, all with holding John's name.

Ω

Everything is set up and ready Friday night and by midday Saturday, the festival is packed. There is a gleam in John's eye as he watches people handing over cash everywhere he looks. He wants to advertise himself and his new church but restrains from letting anybody know that he has anything to do with it. He almost has enough money to get started and isn't going to let anything screw it up now. The festival is such a huge success that John decides to do it every month. Each festival grows bigger and better and brings in more money than the previous one. The festivals even become a great place where young, single, Christian people can hook up, including John who is doing pretty well for himself.

Ω

John is reluctant to do much work to the building until he has the deed in his hand. There is one thing John has built, though. It's a giant wall-sized plaque thanking all major contributors, right inside the main entrance, which everyone passes through to enter the building. There are a handful of names and businesses boldly stamped on the plaque of John's biggest contributors. Contributions can either be monetary or donated time working towards John's goal. John wants to show his appreciation to those who help him so much, and he knows that people will reach a little deeper in their pockets to get their name on the plaque. John also knows quite a few people who will be embarrassed because they have the means to have their name on the plaque, but do not.

Ω

Finally John has enough money to outright buy the property. Of course, between the two churches, John has a couple of lawyers in his pocket. They finalize the sale and set John up with everything he legally needs to operate a church. Although John needs a little more money for renovations and a good start, he relaxes a little bit. Sunday morning he stands before both congregations and holds the deed straight in the air and proclaims, "Praise God we did it. Achieving this almost unattainable goal reassures me that this is what God wants us to do." John has been debating on how and when to drop the bomb on the council. All he knows for sure is that he wants to be there to see the look on their faces. He needs just a little more time yet and decides to keep his cool just a little longer.

Ω

The only thing left to do is some minor renovations to turn the warehouse into a church and a place for John to live. John has enough foresight to have a couple general contractors in his pocket, as well. He even has a sawmill owner and a planning-mill owner lined up which supplies almost all the lumber for practically nothing. They are all eager to get their names and businesses on the plaque. John always saves a chunk of cash for himself in case something goes wrong, but other than that, every single penny that comes in is spent on supplies the next week. The minor renovations are turning into some extravagant building projects, which are pushing the projected start date back weeks at a time. John just keeps telling people, "If your gonna do it, do it right. When it comes to God I'm not half-assing anything."

Ω

By the time everything is ready, both of the unionized churches have been filled to capacity for a few months, and the council still has no idea what is going on. John knows that once he executes his move, the council will never let him back in. He doesn't worry about burning any bridges. He picks a Sunday and informs both congregations that this will be his last sermon in those churches. He will be preaching in his new church the following Sunday, and he hopes to see everyone there. John fantasizes about the council begging him to stay, but when he finally tells them what he is doing, they just snicker at him. One council member speaks up and asks John how he expects to get his own church. John informs him that he already owns a church that is ready to go and his first service is on Sunday. Another council member blurts out, "Who's gonna go to your church." John conceitedly tells them that at least three quarters of both congregations are there to listen to him and not just to go to that particular church. As John walks towards the door he stops and vengefully tells the council that they had a chance to be a part of his church, but they missed their opportunity.

Ω

On the ride home, John is a little disappointed. He wants to see the council squirm, but they are too pigheaded to realize just how much they need him. It's like they are trying to take his satisfaction away from him. John will just have to settle for knowing the heartache that he is causing them instead of seeing it. John figures that even if he takes every member away from them, they probably still will not admit that he has gotten the better of them. John already has his first sermon ready to go, but decides to work on it some more. He wants the first one to be the best yet. Now that he actually has his own church, he focuses on financially hurting the council.

Ω

On opening Sunday, John greets everybody at the door. He is nervously taking inventory on how many of his previous congregation shows up. It's hard to keep track with everyone greeting and congratulating him, but he is pretty sure just about everyone is there. John relaxes a little and concentrates on the delivery of his sermon. After a very powerful and uplifting service filled with laughter and singing, John actually receives a standing ovation. At that moment John knows for sure that his church will be a huge success. It takes about three hours for the last person to leave the church. Everybody wants to talk to John and make diner plans or share new ideas. John is starting to get anxious for people to leave. All he wants to do is have a relaxing evening counting the offering. After counting all the money, John is a little disappointed. He thought there would be more but realizes everybody gave him all that they could afford to start the church. He decides to give them some time to recover before he starts throwing hints that salvation isn't cheap.

Ω

The council has to scurry around to find a replacement for John at the other two churches, but manages to do so without missing a Sunday. The new minister shows up at both places only to preach to a handful of people in each church. The council figures that it is just a fluke, because John's church is the new thing, and there will be some loyal people come back to their church. After a while the council finally comes to grips with the fact that John has taken about ninety-five percent of the congregation that was sitting in their churches a couple of months ago. The council sues John for embezzling church money to start his own church and for soliciting the churches members while he worked for them. John's lawyers are like sharks at the trial and quickly win him the verdict. Mainly because there is no evidence to support embezzling and any money that John receives is a gift. It also isn't against the law for John to salt for members to go to his new church. At the end of the trial John finally gets what he is longing for. John gets to see the pitiful looks on the council members faces as it sinks in that John beat them and is financially costing them dearly.

Ω

John is content with all his hurdles behind him, for now. He is very anxious to see where the future will take him. John is completely unaware of the ravenous monster that he has released into his soul that will never be satisfied. He is quite proud of himself but still lost in his solitude. John has accomplished the first step of many that will lead to a destiny that he may never fully comprehend.

CHAPTER THREE
HOLY STATE

John is well on his way to living his dream, although he is not sure what his dream is. His church is a huge success from the very beginning. John has just about everybody from his previous churches, but his new church is only half full. He has an empty feeling inside of him. The sight of the empty seats in his church greatly disturbs him. He realizes that the more successful he becomes, the more ambitious he becomes and whatever he has is not enough. It's time for another festival, and the organizers want to know if John plans to continue having them. John eagerly decides to continue having them since they are so profitable. This time, John can advertise himself and his new church and hopefully recruit a lot of new members.

Ω

John wants to put a name to his festival, and he realizes that he doesn't even have a name for his church. Since everything going on around John is a new beginning and he has proclaimed in his first sermon that his new church is the start to save the human race, he names his church Eden. He picks Eden because

48

that's where God's chosen people lived in the beginning. He then names his festival *The Sixth Day*, because that was the day of the creation of man. John changes the agenda of the festival and makes himself the center of attention. As each festival becomes larger, so does the attendance at church on Sunday. People even start camping out overnight just so they can attend services in the morning.

Ω

With John's life on easy street and with nothing for him to obsess about, an old demon starts creeping back into his life. This time he has plenty of opportunities to satisfy his desires at the festivals. *The Sixth Day* has become so popular that there are many people starting to come for other reasons than religion. With John becoming somewhat of a local celebrity, it's becoming easier and easier for him to pick up women. There also are more and more women at the festival that's not so virtuous.

At the festival, one of the wives that is shared with John sees him sneaking a young woman into his office late in the evening. The shared wife has become infatuated with John because he has turned into such a rich and powerful man. In a jealous fit, she goes to confront John. Later the woman's husband realizes that he hasn't seen his wife for an hour or so, and he goes to look for her. From down the hall the man sees his wife, John, and the other woman coming out of the office. He can tell just by looking at them exactly what they have been doing. The man becomes furious. First of all, if his wife is involved in a threesome with a man and a woman, he should be the man. Second he feels betrayed by his wife and John. He wants to confront John, but what can he say when he offers his wife to him. The man is also afraid of getting run out of town, probably without his wife, by the congregation who seems like they will do anything to protect John.

Ω

John notices that the couple is not in church the next morning but thinks nothing of it. Later in the week, a newspaper article comes out stating that an inside source revealed that *The Sixth* Day is nothing but a big sex party with John right in the middle of it all. John cannot believe it. He immediately tries to find out who the source is from the newspaper. He figures it's the council, and this time he is going to sue them for slander. The newspaper will not reveal their source but assures John that it is one person and not the council. John begins to wonder if it can be the husband of his threesome partner. The Sunday that they were not in church was the first time they missed since John had known them. John discusses the situation in church. This time the congregation is just as involved as John. It is easy for John to get them riled up and mad at the instigator. If the source is sitting there, he will be afraid of getting tarred and feathered if anyone finds out. It's John's way of warning the person without actually threatening them.

Ω

At the next festival, John realizes that the bad publicity turned out to be good publicity. There are hoards of people rolling in all day long. It's obvious that most of them are looking for a good time and probably never read one single verse from the Bible. John doesn't care as long as they come with lots of money and leave without it. John's people do care though, and they express their feelings to him. John is not happy, but his back is against the wall. He knows that he has to keep his people happy in order to keep them under control. Everybody come up with a compromise to have just one big festival a year, all weekend long. People can camp out all weekend or come as many days as they like. Everybody seems satisfied with the idea but John. The whole reason he started his own church is so he wouldn't have to answer to anyone, and already he has to give in to his people. It seems that John traded in one council for a bigger one.

For the first time John feels like giving up. He thinks about saving up a boatload of money and selling his church. He can live off the money's interest for the rest of his life. That idea does not last very long though. He likes the attention and respect that he receives way too much to give it up. There is still something missing from John's life, and he can't figure out what it is. Eventually John decides that he wants to be married and start a family. Of all the women John has been involved with, there is not one of them that he feels that way about. In fact every time he thinks about marriage or a family, he thinks about Amy. There is only one way to put her out of his mind, so he decides to track her down.

John hires someone to find her and give him her information and address. While he waits, he will not let himself get his hopes up. He expects the worst, that she is happily married with children. Turns out she is married to the same dirt bag she started dating in high school. Amy also has a kid that is age appropriate for what John warned her about. Even though John tried to prepare himself, he is still heartbroken. After awhile John decides to go see where she lives and check things out a little bit, since she is not too far away. When John finds Amy's house, he wonders how someone so pretty and smart with such a bright future ends up living the way she is. She lives in a run-down trailer on the edge of a depressing little town.

John parks in a lot diagonally across the street to watch the place for a while before driving home. As he sits there looking at the dump, he wonders how he can accomplish so much but some loser dirt ball gets what John wants more than anything in the whole world. Amy walks outside with her son to hang clothes on the line. John can hear his own heart beating in his chest as he gazes at her across the street. She isn't quite the vision of beauty that John remembers, but that is just because she is not groomed and wearing raggedy clothes. John is in a trance. watching her do her work. He watches her playing with her son, and she seems truly happy.

John needs to go home and think about things for a while. He doesn't want to interfere with Amy's life if she is happy, but at the same time he is a little jealous that she is happy. Just as John is about to leave an old rust bucket pickup pulls in the driveway. John figures that it must be Amy's husband. He can tell right away that she is not happy to see him. A dirty, greasy man jumps out of the truck, with a beer in his hand, and asks Amy what's for supper. Amy asks him if he has picked up any groceries. The man grumbles something under his breath that John can't hear and starts to work on a racecar that is sitting in the driveway. The racecar is by far the nicest thing on the property. The guy is putting something very shiny under the hood when Amy storms around the corner of the trailer. John can tell they are in a heated argument, but the only thing he can hear is Amy asking the guy what her son is going to eat for supper. The man just grabs her and starts groping and kissing all over her saying, "Aw, come on baby." John can see the disgust on Amy's face as she breaks away and takes her son into the house. John grows very angry and almost takes his car and smashes the guy into the grill of his racecar. John maintains his composure as he thinks that there has to be a better way to help Amy and heads for home to think.

Ω

John doesn't sleep a wink all night. He can't stop thinking about what Amy is going through every minute of every hour. He decides that he is going back the next morning to get Amy out of there. As he is driving to Amy's house the next day, he rehearses what he is going to say to her. When he arrives at the trailer the rusted pickup is sitting in the driveway. John parks in the same lot and waits for her husband to leave. John spends a very long day waiting. Amy's husband never leaves, but John witnesses enough to make him even more determined to rescue her. John heads home with plans of trying again the next day. After another sleepless night and a long day where the husband never leaves, John becomes very frustrated and yells, "Don't this guy ever go to work." He jerks his car into gear and peals out. John heads home again that evening very discouraged. It's the weekend now, and John figures that he will have to wait until the next week to talk to Amy.

Ω

It is the longest weekend of John's life. He keeps imagining the things that the dirt ball is doing to Amy, and it drives John crazy. He is so distracted that a couple of his followers ask if he is all right after church on Sunday. Bright and early Monday morning John heads back down the road towards Amy's house. He arrives just in time to see her husband leave. John waits for about an hour to make sure he doesn't come back. While he is waiting, he rehearses exactly how he will talk Amy into leaving with him. John takes a deep breath, checks his appearance in the rearview mirror and pulls into the driveway. John knocks on the door. Amy opens the door, and they both just blankly stare at each other. For the first time in John's life he is speechless. He can tell Amy is glad to see him, but he can also tell that she is embarrassed. Amy tells John that she is glad to see him. She then apologizes and informs him that he will have to leave as she shuts the door in his face.

John stands on the porch for a while, stunned, trying to gather himself. John beats on the door and yells in that he isn't leaving until she talks to him. Amy reluctantly opens the door and lets him in. Amy introduces John to her son Ben. As John and Amy start catching up, the conversation quickly turns into John's success story. Since John's favorite subject is himself, he is more than eager to tell Amy what he has accomplished and how rich he is. John is finally through, and Amy starts to tell him that when she graduated high school her boyfriend did not want her to go off to college. They got into a big fight until Amy told him that she was going with or without him. Her boyfriend later gave in to her wishes, and they made up. A month later she was pregnant. Amy knew that he was just trapping her, but he talked her into getting married for the baby's sake. He promised her that he would take good care of her and the baby. Amy finishes her story with, "This is as far as we got."

John asks Amy to leave her husband and come live with him. He has all the details worked out. He wants her to leave with him the next day while her husband is at work, leave him a note, and John's lawyers will take care of the divorce. Amy declines his offer because she does not want to break up Ben's home. John cannot care less about the kid. If it were up to him, he would leave Ben there. John can see Amy's unconditional love for Ben though, and he uses that to try to convince her. He tells her that it will be a better life for Ben with food in his belly and decent clothes and shelter. Amy still declines, but John can tell that she is thinking about it. John just gives her his cell phone number and tells her that if she changes her mind or if she ever needs him, to call day or night and he leaves.

Ω

John has given Amy his best sales pitch to make the move, and there is nothing else he can do. He figures he will just drop in about once a week until he convinces her. Two days later, Amy calls John to come and get her. John races to her house and picks her up. She is completely ready to go when John pulls in the driveway. She only has one duffle bag full of things to bring along for her and Ben. John has to stop on the way home for them to get something to eat. John can't believe how they ravish down about two meals apiece. When they get back to the church and settled in, Amy and Ben both fall fast asleep. Five hours later they wake up, and both of them take long hot showers and want to go eat again. John can tell that normal, everyday things that he takes for granted are blessings for them.

Ω

John has his lawyers start working on Amy's divorce right away. As soon as she is divorced, John has every intension on marrying her and adopting Ben. Amy informs him that he cannot adopt Ben. John is not happy at all. Amy tells him that Ben knows who his father is, and it is not anybody else's place to decide if he has a relationship with his father or not. This is a major problem for John. He doesn't want either of them even seeing that scuz-whacker again. John knows deep down that the guy does not want anything to do with his kid and is just using him as a permanent connection to Amy. John is really beside himself when he has to drive Ben to custody visits with his father. Ben's father jumps John and tells him that he isn't Ben's dad and not to lay a finger on him or tell him what to do. That really strikes a nerve with John. John cannot stand a guy like that, thinking that he can tell John what to do. John realizes that it is naive of him to think that he can just whisk Amy and Ben away and that will be the end of it. John starts second guessing himself of whether or not he wants to be involved with Amy. He can't get the thought out of his head about working so hard to get total control of everything, only to have to listen to this loser.

Ω

Things settle down for a few days, until John and Amy awaken around midnight to somebody yelling outside. They run to the window. There is Ben's dad holding a pistol to his head, threatening to blow his brains out unless Amy comes home. Amy tells John to call the police while she goes to make sure Ben does not see or hear what is going on. Amy knows that he is drunk. If he gets arrested, at least he will be safe until he sobers up. After enough time has passed for the police to get there, and nobody shows up, Amy returns to the window to see what is going on. John does not hear her coming. She hears John saying under his breath, "Nobody knows how much I want you to pull the trigger." Amy yells at John and asks if he called the police. John replies a very calm no, and Amy quickly dials 911. After the police come and arrest Ben's father, John and Amy get into a huge fight.

Ω

John can hear the buzz of rumors floating around through the congregation about the new woman and child that are staying at the church. Everybody also knows that the police were there and arrested someone. John decides to give an explanation of the situation. He simply tells his followers, in the middle of his church service, that Amy is an old friend that he is helping. John goes on to say that Amy and Ben were in a home with a very abusive man. John raises his head slightly and informs everybody that he rescued them. The whole congregation blesses John like he is a saint, while Amy just sits there mortified. After the service is over, Amy thanks John for making her and Ben look like total losers in front of five hundred people. Another argument ensues. In fact, it seems that all they do is argue.

Ω

Things are not so good in the newly formed family. John is impatient and rough on Ben. Ben is old enough to have picked up some of his father's mannerisms, which drives John crazy. Just looking at Ben is a constant reminder of his father. John and Amy are not very compatible living under the same roof, either. It seems like everything that each one does, gets on the other one's nerves. Finally they decide that it isn't going to work. John still cares enough for Amy to not let her go back to where she was, so he sets her up to start over. Amy receives free schooling, rent, and free childcare, plus John sends her a few hundred dollars a week until she gets on her feet.

Ω

John's relationship with Amy, not working, is a major blow to his emotional state. John starts to lose faith, and questions his goals in life. He can't understand how he can get the one thing he always wanted the most, and once he has her, he can't stand her. John has always held hope for him and Amy no matter what, but now it's final. It's like losing a part of his entire life. John almost feels as if Amy had died.

What is the sense of becoming rich and powerful if there is no one to share it with? Over five hundred people utterly love John, but he feels completely alone. John becomes depressed and starts mopping around. He isn't putting much into his sermons, and he starts lying around with women again. For the first time since John started preaching, his congregation does not seem to be growing.

Ω

A wanna-be entrepreneur in John's congregation approaches him with an idea to make some extra cash. He wants to video John's sermons, make copies, and sell them over the Internet. John knows the guy is just trying to get a piece of John's success, but if he is willing to do all of the work, John is willing to take half the profits. John does not think the venture will be very successful, but he starts putting a little more effort into his sermons. John likes thinking of himself as a sellable product. All it takes is selling the first couple hundred videos and John is transformed into a superstar in front of the camera. It's not long until they are selling more copies than they can make in a week's time.

With the success of the videos comes John's biggest opportunity. Out of the blue, a local television station approaches John about airing his services live every Sunday morning. Being on TV is all John needs to get completely out of his funk. John agrees to the TV station's offer with a gleam in his eye and leaves his old business partner in the dust. John starts writing sermons like never before. His church is only about three quarters full, so he goes out and hires people to attend church in order to make the church look packed on TV. John only wants three things out of life, money, power, and Amy and if he can't have them all, he is going to have as much as possible. TV has become John's new passion. If the people can't come to church, then John will be in their living rooms. John fantasizes about being the number one preacher in the nation. He knows that fame will automatically bring him money and power, and the three of those will bring him another Amy.

Ω

Meanwhile the first annual three-day festival is drawing near. There is a huge field across the creek that is the property line between the church and the farm. John approaches the farmer about leasing the field for the festival. John waves some cash in front of the farmer's face, and he reluctantly agrees to the lease.

John has it all planned out. Campers and tents will be in the field, and food and entertainment on the church side. John has a couple of small footbridges built so the people can cross the creek. John goes all out on advertising and even buys some airtime at the TV station. The festival will be the biggest event the local area has ever seen.

Ω

The first campers start rolling in later Friday morning. They keep coming all day, and by Friday evening there is a line of traffic backed up the road trying to get in. Around ten o'clock Friday night, an ambulance has to be called for a drug overdose. Early Saturday morning, it becomes clear that it is going to be sweltering hot. By noon, people are jumping of the footbridges and skinny-dipping in the creek. All the church members have a look of sheer terror on their faces as they wonder what they have gotten themselves into. By Saturday evening, there are two more drug overdoses. It's just getting dark and a man, who has been attending the festivals since the beginning and has become pretty good friends with John, finds him to say goodbye. John asks him why he is not staying for church in the morning. The man tells John that he is sorry, but there are people all over the field having sex. The dope smoke is so thick that he is catching a buzz, and he's getting his family out of there. John feels bad about his friend having to leave but there is so much money rolling in that he quickly gets over it.

Ω

The festival is finally over, and the aftermath of cleaning-up starts. It's a weeklong project that people work on when they have spare time. It gives John good one on one time with his followers. But every one of them tells John that they are glad it's over, and they never want to experience anything like that again. John is stunned and does not want to hear that. He leaves the first half dozen or so comments go. After that, he figures that he had better nip it in the bud. He is already looking forwards to and making plans for the next year. John starts telling the complainers that they all started their church because they do not want someone else telling them how to worship God. He then asks if they are going to become what they despise and start dictating how people are going to worship at their church. When John tells people that, they look at him like they know that is just a lame excuse for condoning what went on. Clean-up is about wrapped up. John is having the same conversation with a group of his followers, when one of them speaks up and asks why they need all that money anyhow. Another one speaks up and says, "It has to be way more than we need." John spouts off silently inside his mind, *more money than WE need. It's **my** church, **my** festival.* For the first time John separates himself from his congregation. John realizes that there will always be somebody questioning his methods.

Ω

62

John has a very uneasy feeling. He always has control of his people. They would always do anything he asks, but lately it's as if they are doubting him. John comes to the conclusion that one problem is that his people are influenced too much by the outside world. His people spend all but about two hours every Sunday in the outside world. John decides that he needs more time with them. He also knows that he will have to start spending more money on charities and helping the needy to keep suspicions down. Everything settles down, and everybody's life returns to normal and John spends a lonely week sitting by himself in his church. He is going stir crazy. He even starts thinking of reasons that he needs to go visit people just to talk to someone. He makes up some committees, which holds weekly meetings at the church, and starts a Wednesday night Bible study.

Ω

A few weeks quickly pass by, and John now has some things to occupy his time. First, the farmer that leased the field for the festival visits John and tells him that he will not be able to lease the field again because of liability purposes. He tells John that the extra money is nice, but he and his wife are getting old and all they have is the farm. One lawsuit and they will lose everything. John is mad at the farmer but understands. John does not even know if he can talk his people into another festival or not. Then John receives a letter from the township stating that he does not have the proper permits for his festival. He tries to obtain everything he needs, but all he gets is the runaround. He has to write out a check for this and that and wait and wait until he receives one permit before he can apply for another. The township denies the last permit and refunds his money with no explanation. John tries to get his money back for the others, but he can't because he has those permits. It's bad enough that they stuck their noses in and stopped John's festival, but the kicker is that they swindled him out of a few hundred dollars to do it.

The crippling blow to John is when he receives notification that he is being audited. Being a non-profit organization, the church does not have to pay taxes, but John does. The government wants to make sure they are getting their fair share and John is not ripping them off, which he is. The end result of this fiasco is John having to open another account in Eden Church's name and transferring most of his money into it to avoid paying a fortune in back taxes with interest. He also has to name a treasurer and president who will be authorized to use the account. John ponders long and hard of who to give joint custody of his money. He finally picks the two that he feels are the most loyal to him and enters their names on the proper paperwork. John never tells either one of them about their new positions or that they have the ability to write checks out of a seven figure account.

Ω

Never before has John felt so helpless and alone. He feels like he is being tortured, having accomplished everything he wants in life so quickly only to have it all taken away even faster. John has the spirit sucked right out of him, and he gives up. He does have a plan to come out financially set for life, though.

First, he gives himself a big raise and just flat out starts paying more taxes. He is still bringing in money hand-over-fist from offerings, and people all over TV land are now sending him money. John is still sole owner of the land and building that is Eden Church. He decides to hang in there until he has lived on the property long enough that he will not have to pay capital gain tax, then sell the property to the church for an outrageous price and get his money back scot-free.

Ω

John is busy trying to keep himself busy. He is so lonely in that huge church all by himself that he is thinking about dating a plain-looking young woman in his congregation who has been throwing herself at him since the very beginning. He has the phone in his hand to call the girl just so he will not have to eat dinner alone again. There is a knock at the door. John opens the door, and there stands a scruffy, young girl. One look and John can tell she is homeless. Her hair is all matted, and her clothes are torn and dirty. The girl asks John if he knows where someone in trouble might get some help. John is a pro at helping people who are abused by life. John simply says, "Yes" and takes the girl by the arm and leads her in the door. He shows her where she can shower and takes her to a back room where the church stores donated clothes for the poor. John tells her to try and find something to wear, and he will be back in a little while with supper for them.

Ω

When John gets back, the girl is sitting at the table looking like a beaten dog. John sits a few bacon cheeseburgers and a pile of greasy French fries down on the table. The feeding frenzy begins. John notices that beneath all that crust, the young girl is very pretty. He then remembers having a short conversation with her at the last festival. John has just bathed, clothed and fed the girl without even asking a question. He knows not to pressure the girl, so he starts talking about himself and his church. It only takes about half an hour for John to gain the girl's total trust. She begins spilling her guts to John, telling him everything. She is a sixteen-year-old runaway with a sad story. After she finishes eating, John takes her to a spare bedroom and fixes her up a bed for a much needed good night's sleep.

Ω

The girl wakes the next morning to a huge breakfast that John has made for her. After she eats, John tells her that she is welcome to stay as long as she wants, if she agrees to say that she lied about her name, age, and family. She agrees, and John picks Grace for her fake name. She likes the name and has a smile on her face as she begins to do some chores that John thought up for her to do. John wishes he could tell her to go home, but there is no way he can do that. He does eventually talk her in to calling her mother and letting her know that she is all right and staying at a church-run halfway house.

John and Grace quickly become the best of friends. They have some kind of emotional connection, and John is starting to develop feelings for her. Grace is an attractive girl, and John has noticed, but he has no interest in her that way. He truly is just trying to help her. The only thoughts John has about Grace is to be her friend until she turns eighteen, and then see where their relationship goes from there. John does have strong convictions against men taking advantage of young, vulnerable girls. The situation with Grace gives John a good idea of actually starting a no-questions-asked halfway house to help anybody in need that can find their way to him. John and Grace work side-by-side researching and developing plans to make it happen. John is growing closer to her every day.

Ω

Grace's mother eventually sees her on TV, sitting in John's church. The police arrive later in the afternoon and take John and Grace both in for questioning. Everybody automatically assumes that John is a pedophile, and he knows it, too. John tries to tell the police what the real danger in Grace's life is, but nobody believes him. John never has laid a finger on Grace, and he is later released. A social worker comes to the police station and takes Grace back to her home. John is devastated to lose what he thinks is his soul-mate. John's heart breaks every time he thinks about the stories that Grace has told him about her home life. He knows full well that they are all happening again. Two weeks pass by, and Grace's stepfather rapes her for the last time. She gets a shotgun out of the closet and blows his head clear off. Grace then sticks the barrel in her mouth and pushes the trigger with a pencil. When Grace pushes on the trigger, she cocks her head to the side a little to reach. She survives the initial blast. She is in critical condition at the hospital with half a face and the other half of her body paralyzed.

John comes to visit her every day. He is the only one. Grace's mother blames her for leading her husband on. Grace lay in agony for two weeks before she succumbs to her injuries with John by her side.

Ω

This is the final straw for John. He is consumed by anger, grief and emotions he doesn't even understand. Although John knows that the people who took Grace from him were only trying to help her, he still blames them for her death. He truly wants to kill everybody involved in sending Grace home. John just wants to be left alone. The more successful he becomes the more people stick their nose in his business. John has been tinkering with an idea for some time now, and he decides to go for it. John goes to see his neighbor, the farmer, and asks to buy his farm. The farmer just snickers and shakes his head until John makes an offer. It only takes about thirty seconds for the farmer to sell out at that price. John now will own all five hundred acres behind his church. He plans to start his own private church community. Grace was passionate about the halfway house, and John is going to follow it through in her honor. This time, it will be inside a sanctuary where nobody can interfere. John figures if everybody lives, works and worships together with minimal influence from the outside world, things will be much better. John has gone from starting his own church to starting his own religion. All government agencies will have to respect their religious freedom. John thinks that it's the only way that he can have total control, plus he will never be alone again.

Ω

John spends weeks walking the farm with a gleam of revenge in his eye. An unquenchable thirst for power sparks his imagination. The vision of John's empire starts to appear around him. John runs to start construction, but he hesitates. He will have to be careful. The government will shut him down before Eden has a chance. The more inconspicuous and self-sufficient they are, the better the community will be. John restrains himself to the open fields to think. As he lay in the grass, starring into the blue sky, he wonders how he will convince his people to live and work inside of Eden. A dark, storm cloud slowly consumes the sky. John can feel that Judgment Day is coming, sooner than he thinks. Eden will rise above the destruction, with John at the helm to lead the new world.

CHAPTER FOUR
RIGHT HAND OF GOD

John eagerly starts to ask some of his people to abandon their lives and live in the community. He can see the fear in their eyes and quickly realizes that this will be his biggest challenge yet. John grits his teeth in anger as people stare at him, with pity consuming their faces. It's clear that they all think he is insane. He wants to lash out at them, but he knows to tread lightly and be patient. John will have to hone all of his skills to convince his congregation that they want to serve him.

There are only a few people that give John a hint of interest in the community. John knows that it will be hard to convince the ones with nice houses and good jobs. Most will never make the move no matter what. John realizes the fact that no matter how devout his people are they will never trade in their pampered and successful lifestyles for God. John notices a slight decline in the offering on Sunday. He is not too concerned because his TV church-goers are sending in more and more money every week. He knows that he has spooked his followers. Many of John's people are still wandering where he got the money to buy the farm. John is prepared for conflict between his church and his community. He decides to keep them separate and even makes plans for another simple church inside the community.

Ω

John's first priority is getting the halfway house operational. He feels that he owes it to Grace. He also wants to show everyone that his intensions are good, and he is helping people, not trying to be the monarch of his own kingdom. Since John's church turned out so nice, he builds everything in the same fashion. He erects large steel buildings then makes the insides suit the purpose. Nobody on the outside will know what the buildings are or what is going on inside them. The average person probably will not even give the buildings a second look, thinking they are just hog or chicken barns. When the halfway building is erected, rooms are partitioned off inside with a bed, shower, sink and toilet in them. It's basically a very cheap, chintzy motel, but it's free, and to a homeless person, it is luxury.

After a fully stocked mess hall is completed, John hits the road advertising his sanctuary and handing out cards to anybody who looks like they need a break. It's not long until people start showing up. They are invited to be part of John's family, as he starts calling it. All they have to do is work within the community, and they will be completely taken care of. Most join the family, some move on, and the rest are lazy freeloaders who are thrown out. John gives every single person who asks a second chance but has no tolerance for anybody not willing to help themselves. Word spreads like wildfire. Every teenager with a troubled home life for a hundred miles in every direction is hitchhiking towards Eden.

Ω

John has managed to talk some of his congregation into making the move. They sell their homes and any unnecessary possessions and give the money to John. Even though the church and community are kept separate, the money is not. John considers it all to be his, anyhow. Private housing is constantly being constructed. Housing is basically comfortable apartments built inside the same steel buildings. John's private community is underway. If the men and women of the congregation who make the move have good jobs, they are allowed to keep them. John makes them take a vow never to discuss anything about the family in the outside world. They all just give their paycheck to John, and he takes care of all their needs. It actually is a very stress-free lifestyle with no worries about paying bills or any other of life's struggles.

Ω

John still worries about outside influences on his family. He has to let certain people go out and work for income. It's expensive supporting all those people. He knows that his original congregation who wants no part of the community will eventually get tired of supporting it. Very young people are showing up left and right with no marketable skills whatsoever other than doing chores and busywork inside the community. These youngsters are very draining on the finances, but John loves them because they have not yet developed their own personalities or values. John can mold them by his ideals. He automatically assumes that he is the perfect father figure for the troubled teens. John racks his brain for another way to convince some more influential people to join his family.

Ω

John keeps preaching about the end of the world. He asks his congregation during his sermons if they are sure that they are saved. Then, he begs them to make sure if they have any doubt. Of course, John is putting doubt into their heads every other Sunday. John tells them that he is sure the end is near and, if they do not see it, their children or grandchildren will. Now is the time to prepare for it. John corners the ones he wants in his family in a private conversation and invites them to join. He tells them that he believes God is guiding him to prepare a group of survivors to start over in the world. The whole time John acts as if it is a big secret, and he is giving the person that he is talking to a chance of a lifetime.

Ω

The thought of the end of the world scares a handful more to join the family, but still John needs more. John researches how other religious sects before his has pulled off what he is trying to do. He comes up with an idea. He makes it acceptable to have multiple wives inside his community as long as they are of legal age. The marriages are not legal. John just performs a simple ceremony, and all the spouses just live the part. John explains his decision simply by saying that is why God has more women on earth than men. Also, God said to go forth and multiply, and that is the fastest way to do it in order to repopulate the world. John is good at taking words right out of the Bible and twisting them around and interpreting them to whatever best suites his people, or him. This gets the attention of every man in the church and is also a good way to keep control of the men that John already has. Men will do John's bidding like mindless puppets just for the sheer possibility of having multiple wives.

The only problem left is that most of the women are not so keen on the idea of having sister wives. John starts preaching that women are to be subservient to their husbands, but in the same breath will say that husbands should treat their wives as precious gems and shower them with love and attention. Then he declares that the original wives of the men will not work and be the head of the household. All the secondary wives will do all the work and cater to the first wives like they are queens. Since all the available women were young and homeless, they are easy to control. As long as they are getting some attention or not being abused, they are happy. This leaves a lot of the women more open to the idea of joining the family.

John even takes a couple of young wives himself, to set an example. He also decides that he wants to have some children. John researched and talked about the end of the world so much that he is starting to believe it. He also starts believing that all his thoughts and actions are under the influence of God.

John begins to tell people that whenever a thought enters his head out of the blue, it is God talking to him. John considers himself to be the right hand of God. John wants his own children to take over for him when he is gone, heirs to the throne, one might say. When God destroys the world and spares John's family to start life over, there will need to be someone to lead the people after John is gone. It's as if John is striving for immortality of his accomplishments and power that he has obtained on earth.

John wastes no time in starting to have children with his wives. He really steps up to the plate every night with one of his wives or both or sometimes both at the same time. He has no reservations about getting them pregnant right away. If they become unappealing and strapped with a kid, John can simply take a new wife. A few months pass by and neither of John's wives is pregnant. John has told a lot of people that he is trying to have children and now he is embarrassed. Not being able to get one wife pregnant is one thing, but not being able to get two pregnant, then everybody knows who is at fault. John becomes paranoid that everybody he talks to is thinking about his inadequacies. He starts trying harder and even tries every trick in the book to conceive. John is under so much stress to get the job done that he is not even enjoying all of the trying.

There are already babies being born in the community. John becomes very spiteful when he has to pay for the birth of other people's children when he can't have any of his own. Having babies is expensive and none of the men's health insurance from their jobs will pay for medical expenses for a woman who is not legally their spouse. John decides to build a health clinic complete with supplies, midwives and nurses to deliver babies and to treat minor health problems. John adopts a policy that if a woman or her child gets into trouble during childbirth, it's God's will. Nature will be left to take its course. It's a cruel and harsh pill to swallow in today's world, but everybody accepts it. John easily recruits a couple of doctors who has lost just about everything to their ex-wives. Stress-free living, doing what they love to do, and the promise of as many young women as they want, which is what got them into trouble to begin with, is all they need to hear.

Ω

John's family is growing by leaps and bounds. For the first time since it started, it's becoming financially stable. Everybody seems to be very happy and everything is working like clockwork. John is pleased with his community, but there is still an important piece missing from his life. John never worried too much about having his own children, but now that he can't, he wants one more than anything. He has his eye on a young girl who he's been waiting for. John is going to try to have a child with her as soon as she is old enough. He figures that all he can do is to keep trying with as many women as he can and hopefully find the right combination for success. John tells the young women who they are to marry in order to keep everyone happy. He gives his most influential men the pick of the litter. John has to be patient and wait his turn for another wife. He knows that he only has control if his family is happy. There are a lot of young men who are getting tired of a celibate lifestyle and some are starting to leave. John is not so much worried about them leaving as much as he is about the possibility of them talking to the outside world. He comes up with the solution of assigning the young men to the older, legally married women to do with what they please. This keeps everybody happy for now, except John. He is getting a little fed up with bending over backwards to keep the peace. He starts to wonder if he even has control.

Ω

Early one morning, John wakes to find that a small army of police and governments agents has completely surrounded Eden. A column of SUVs and assault vehicles drive through town right to John's doorstep. John storms out the door demanding to know what is going on. He is met by a skinny man about six foot six wearing a suit and sunglasses. The agent hands John a search warrant while identifying himself and explaining the contents of the warrant. This infuriates John to the point that he gets in the guy's face and demands that he leave his property immediately. The agent is obviously peeved, and he tells John it's only his property if the government lets it be his property. The agent turns and gives the signal. His men begin tearing through John's town like a tornado. John asks the agent what they are looking for, and the agent simply states, "guns, drugs, and abused minors." John tells him that he will find nothing of the sort here and that it is a religious community. The agent turns and glares at John saying, "We know this is an organized town of pedophiles." John's first instinct is to take a swing at the agent and call his family to arms to stop the search. John knows that it's a battle he can't win and would probably be the end of his town right then and there.

Ω

After the agents and police search every corner of every building, the only thing they find is a handful of minors listed as missing. When the agent in charge questions John about them, he states that he has no idea who they are or how old they are. John tells the agent that the church is only operating a shelter for homeless and abused people. The agent informs John there will be an investigation. As he starts walking towards his vehicle he tells John that they are watching him. A couple of vans pull up and the missing teenagers are loaded up to be taken back to their homes. There is the girl that John had his eye on for months, along with a couple other promised brides being loaded into the van. John becomes infuriated and charges the agent yelling, "You can't send them back to be abused." John reaches the agent and he grabs his arm, spinning him around to make him listen. The agent instinctively drives his elbow and forearm into John's chest knocking him clean off his feet and flat on his back.

John just sits in the grass trying to catch his breath, watching as the intruders speed off in a cloud of dust. John looks around, and everybody is just standing there starring at him with blank faces. He struggles to his feet and storms back into the house. He locks himself in a room as his mind races back and forth about what has just happened. John is embarrassed and wants to kill the agent who had hit him.

He is also mad at his family for not helping him or even asking if he is all right. John screams as loud as he can and asks God why he keeps letting people interfere with his work. John can see very clearly that there is always going to be somebody more powerful than him that will try and keep him beat down. John can't see that the main concern is the welfare of the teenagers. He takes everything personally, thinking that it's a direct attack on him.

Ω

John becomes discouraged and depressed again. He really does think that God will destroy the world and spare him and his family. Maybe it's just wishful thinking to get back at everybody who has crossed him. He decides to just lay low and wait for it to happen. He has a pretty good life, which is far better than most people dream of. He will just have to follow the laws and take his lumps whenever he has too. John really tries, but the more he thinks about things the madder he gets, and he can't stop thinking about things. As long as John keeps busy doing something, he is all right. If he has any idle time, he automatically starts obsessing about things. It's worse at night, which keeps him from sleeping most of the night. He quickly becomes sleep deprived. One night, he lay in bed stewing and becomes so angry that he leaps straight out of bed ready to kick somebody's ass. There is nobody there, so he trashes his room to release his anger. After it's all over, he sits there alone in the dark thinking about all the times before when he overcame his obstacles. Then he decides that he can do it again. He will go straight to the top.

Ω

John studies and researches all aspects of the government, from the local level to the national. He makes another list of every politician, law enforcement and military leader that will benefit his cause. Now all he has to do is convince them to support him. If he can pull this one off, there will be nobody to stop him from doing whatever he wants. John already knows how to convince these men. He will use the same incentive that he used to convince the successful members of his church to move to his town, as many young girls, or boys, as they like. The only problem is getting a chance to approach these people. John figures that the easiest people to meet with will be the politicians. If he gains their support, they will supply John with the rest. No politicians will give John the time of day until they find out how many loyal followers he has, mostly due to his TV audience.

Ω

John offers the politicians whatever they want. He will let them come and go as they please and will betroth girls as young as fourteen to them. John builds houses for them, and the young girls live there and wait for the politicians to visit. John considers them full members of his family and justifies their absences to the other family members as being important people with important jobs. John still proclaims that the girls have to be of legal age to marry the men. The girls living in the men's houses are just long engagements. What happens behind closed doors, John knows nothing about and cannot be held accountable for. John knows, and so does everybody else, that all he is doing is bribing some of the nation's most powerful men to stay off his back. John has to fight off the sick feeling that he has in his stomach every time a politician visits and disappears into the house with the under-aged girls. Every time he feels that he cannot let it happen, but he feels that he has no choice. It's working and the investigation against John is dropped.

$$\Omega$$

Things are getting back on track for John and his family again. John is getting more and more politicians and law enforcement agents in his pocket. He feels like a mob boss paying off the police with the most valuable thing he has. John has always felt that money would be what gives him the most power, but he finds out that there are always people over him with all the money they need. John discovers that he has the one thing that is more valuable than gold. It's only three feet off the ground, but it rules the world. He quickly realizes that the younger they are the more valuable they are, which John hates, but everybody has to make sacrifices for the cause. When John starts justifying sins to do God's work, he finds himself in a place that he promised himself he would never go. John comforts himself by believing that God will reward those who sacrifice themselves for him.

Ω

All the greedy new members of the family are taking
a toll on the inventory of young eligible wives. Many
of the original family members are unhappy with taking a backseat to John's new alliance with the government. Young people are just not showing up at
Eden fast enough for John to distribute them equally.
For the first time, John puts more importance on
somebody else other than his loyal followers who
have been with him from the beginning. A twenty-
year-old woman shows up at Eden seeking sanctuary
from an abusive relationship. She is a plain-looking
girl, and there does not seem to be much interest in
her except for John. To John, the girl just looks like
a mother if he has ever seen one, and he takes it as a
sign. He wastes no time in sweeping the emotional-
ly-scarred woman off her feet. This one is John's,
and he does not care who does not like it. He is tired
of everybody whining around to him about everything under the sun anyhow. John considers himself
the father of the family but did not anticipate a bunch
of adults acting like children.

Ω

John is quickly married to his third wife. His first
impression of his new wife was correct, and she becomes pregnant within a couple of months. John is
ecstatic and no one can wipe the smile off his face.
Now that John has someone to pass his life's work on
to, he really begins focusing on the future again.
John was starting to think that there is no use pushing

so hard to accomplish so much when he will just eventually die. Everybody will forget all about him, while someone else steps right into his shoes. When the end of the world does come, it will be a new beginning for the people of Eden and John and his offspring will be in charge of the whole country, maybe even the whole world. It's as if John wants the world to come to an end. You can see it in his eyes when he talks about it.

Ω

One of John's main objectives is for Eden to be totally self-sufficient. When God destroys the rest of the world, you will not be able to run to the store to buy food or flick a switch on for electricity. Eden also needs better and more medical capabilities. John's newfound friends from the government also want Eden cut off from the outside world as much as possible. They can only do so much if John and his family are drawing attention to themselves. They especially do not want young pregnant girls showing up at the hospital in desperate need of medical attention. John is more willing to spend money now that he and his child will directly benefit from it.

Ω

One of the first things John builds is a huge warehouse. Inside he starts storing anything he can think of that his family might someday need. John hoards up barrels of fuel, guns and ammunition, building supplies, water, dried and canned food, clothing and even every how-to manual he can find. If John does not have a professional in all the careers he thinks will be useful, he finds one. Then all the people of Eden who do not have jobs either volunteer or are assigned to all the trades. There are farmers to grow food and raise animals. Windmills are erected and generators installed for electricity. Since John's child is about to be born, he steps up the medical facility and staff along with pharmaceuticals. John's wife is the first one to benefit from the new ultrasound machine, and John is having a boy.

John is overjoyed that he is having a son. He is like an ancient emperor building an extravagant city, but he still finds the time to badger his pregnant wife about taking care of his unborn son. All of a sudden she goes into labor about a month early, but the doctor does not seem concerned. After several hours of excruciating pain, John can tell by the look on the doctor's face that something is terribly wrong. The doctor pulls John aside and tells him that he has to get his wife and baby to a hospital immediately. The doctor then explains how the baby is in distress, and he is not equipped to do the procedure to save them both. He tells John that if he saves the baby, there is a good chance that the mother will die. John feels like he is in a bad dream and it's not real. He thinks about his government protectors getting angry if he goes to the hospital. There had been a couple of infants who did not make it before because of John's policy of God's will. If he does not follow his own rules, then nobody else will either. John's hands are tied, and he tells the doctor to do what he can for them both, but save his son. The doctor follows John's orders and cuts the baby out. The mother gets to hold her son for about thirty seconds before she bleeds out and dies. Then the doctor notices that the baby is having troubles breathing. John watches for half an hour while the doctor frantically works on his son, until he dies.

Ω

John just stands there, looking at his son like it's not real. The doctor kicks open the door in a fit of rage and screams as he leaves the room. A few seconds later the doctor storms back in and says, "God's will or not, I can't stand around and watch innocent people die when I know I can help them". The doctor then informs John that he is leaving Eden. John is in such a state of shock that he does not even hear anything the doctor is saying. An hour later, the doctor walks out of Eden with his two wives and nothing but the clothes on their backs, never to be seen again.

Ω

John stands like a statue in his makeshift ER holding his dead son. It all happened so fast that John is having trouble comprehending what has just happened. Many people try to comfort him, but he is completely unresponsive. John holds his dead son for about eight hours. He finally lays his son down, curses God at the top of his lungs and locks himself in his office. Nobody sees or hears from John for days, until he emerges on Sunday morning for church. John stands firm to his convictions and preaches about staying focused, committed, and accepting God's will. John can find an advantage in any situation and decides to make himself an example for his people to follow. He stands before his people reciting his sermon like a robot. The congregation buzzes with comments of John's mental state. It seems like he is dead inside. After church, John eats lunch with his family and goes straight back to his office and locks the door behind him.

John just sits motionless in his office staring at the wall while he thinks for days. He enters a very dark and disturbing place in his mind. Maybe it's the lack of sleep and food or maybe just the extreme emotional distress, but John starts to have terrifying hallucinations. He finally dozes off but quickly awakens from horrible nightmares about his childhood. He does not understand the nightmares because he does not remember most of his early life. John is lying on the floor with his eyes closed trying to get a grip on reality. He hears a voice calling his name. He opens his eyes to see fluffy, white clouds swirling around on the ceiling. John gazes into the white void and starts to float through the clouds. Eden slowly appears through the clouds. John floats closer and closer until a glistening but frightful palace appears towering over the town. John again hears a familiar voice calling his name. He sees Grace and his infant son reaching out for him from a balcony high up on the palace. John stretches his arms out towards them but stops a couple feet short. He looks around and realizes that he is standing on the floor and their hands are in the ceiling. John starts to climb up on his desk to reach them. All of the people who have interfered with him before, start surfacing out of the floor like it's water. They are grabbing hold of John's ankles to pull him back down. John is now sitting on his desk kicking off all of the hands. He manages to break free. Just as he is about to stand up on his desk, a huge red demon-like hand shoots up out of the floor, sinks its claws into John's shoulder and rips him off the desk and on to the floor with a bone-crushing thud.

Ω

John is lying on the floor with the wind knocked out of him. He realizes the floor is very solid, and there is nothing at all on the ceiling. He is scared as hell, and he struggles to his feet and runs right out the door. He does not stop running until he is standing in the middle of town. As he looks around, everything is spinning. John feels severe hunger pains, so he staggers to the mess hall to eat. He stuffs himself with food and water and makes his way back home. He showers and then passes out on the bathroom floor. When he finally awakes his dizziness is gone. He realizes that it's Saturday morning, and he does not have a sermon for church on Sunday. As John walks back to his office to work on a sermon, he re-members all his dreams and hallucinations quite vi-vidly. He knows none of it really happened, but still he opens the office door very slowly and peeks in.

Once inside his office, John calms down and be-gins thinking of a quick and easy sermon for the next morning. He can't focus on his work though. He can't stop thinking about his dead son. He needs someone to blame. He can't blame himself, so he starts thinking about everybody who has pushed him to the point where his child could not be born in a hospital. Everyone who ever denied him or inter-fered with his mission is to blame. The more he thinks about it, the angrier he becomes. Although John is a free man, he can't help but notice that there is always someone in his business telling him what he can or cannot do. It cost him his son's life, and it has to be stopped.

John is also thinking about his dreams and hallucinations. They must have some meaning behind them, but John can't figure it out. Could he really have been suffocated as an infant and strapped to a bed as a toddler? Was his physical deformity purposely inflicted on him? If it were, what possible reason would someone have for doing that? Who is the grinning, deviate-looking man with a pentacle tattooed on his chest standing behind a beautiful but sad-looking naked woman chained to the scorched ground? The demon hand that came out of the floor and jerked John from Grace and his son's reach had to be Satan himself. The only explanation John can come up with is that God has chosen him to be the savior of the world. All those who interfere are under the control of the Devil. John has defeated all of Satan's pawns, and now he has to defeat Satan.

If Satan defeats John, God can't destroy the world and that cannot happen. John becomes more determined than ever to succeed with his plans and be ready for God to make his move. John wonders how God will do it. He would like to be able to look into his enemies' eyes as they die. He starts fantasizing about God giving him the power to destroy the sinners of the world. John envisions lightning bolts shooting from his hands and striking his enemies. On second thought, that is too quick and easy for them. It would be better if God would give him super strength so that he could slowly squeeze their heads until they popped. Or very slowly push a dagger through their chest and into their hearts so they would have time to realize that they are going to hell and John is the one sending them there.

Ω

Suddenly, John has a revelation that God is trying to tell him what to do. God wants to destroy the world through John. John will be God's right hand smashing out sin throughout the world. How on earth will John and his small town of followers conquer the whole world? John begins thinking about how to accomplish the task that has been given to him. He has full confidence that God will put all of the answers into his head. John is up all night thinking and fantasizing when he realizes that the sun is coming up, and he has nothing prepared for church. John is so excited about his new mission that he decides to skip church for the first time since he became a preacher. He calls an old friend to read some scripture and cover for him because he has fallen ill.

Ω

While everybody is at church, John sneaks out and gathers up as much food and water as he can carry back to his office. He knows that he will need all of his strength to pull off his next task. He sits in front of his computer for hours thinking and researching his ideas. John eventually comes up with a basic plan. It will have to be done in steps, but done quickly enough that he will not lose the element of surprise. John will start with his own country, which is probably the most powerful country in the world, but may be the easiest to gain control of. What better place to pick a fight than in your own back yard, plus he will have the element of complete surprise. He will just have to move through the rest of the world fast enough that they will not have time to prepare after they figure out what is going on. If he conquers his own country, he will also have his countries resources to use against the rest of the world.

John just has to figure out how to bring the country to its knees. No matter what, John knows that he will need an army. If he puts the most advanced weapons in the hands of every man in Eden, he still will not have much of one. Even if he has a sizable army, he will not be able to go toe to toe with the nation's military. He will have to even the playing field somehow. If he can sabotage and disable the military, he could possibly have a chance to overthrow the government. John finally realizes that he and his family will have to become terrorists, but only in a much larger scale than the world has ever seen before with one perfectly timed strike. After much research on the world's terrorist activity, John decides that the weapon of choice will be biological warfare. It is the only way that a bunch of people who can't fight their way out of a wet paper bag will have a chance of wiping out the military.

John is smart enough to know that even the best plan will still have some holes in it. He will still need to use force. He thinks about trying to make contact with some of the world's most notorious terrorist groups for help, but then he thinks better of it. They will be hard to control, especially if John succeeds in overthrowing the country. John figures that if he is going to do this, he is going to be in complete control and not put himself in a position to be double-crossed and stabbed in the back when it's all over. He then thinks about hiring mercenaries, but John figures that if things ever looked bad they would skip out on him in a heartbeat. After all, if John goes down, they wouldn't get paid. One thing that John has observed is that most of today's armies do not fight with their hearts like they have for thousands of years before. If the few soldiers of today that do fight for what they believe in had the financial backing, they would rule the world. John is fantasizing about going back in time and cloning a Spartan when it hits him. Maybe he can clone an army. He can find someone who will follow orders with no questions asked and willing to give their lives for a cause. Like a terrorist, or maybe even anybody if the clones wouldn't have any previous mentality. John can brainwash them just like he does with all the teenagers that show up at Eden.

Ω

John thinks the clones are a good idea, but deep down he figures that it will be financially impossible. Even though he is bringing in tens of thousands of dollars every week, every penny will be accounted for. John has accomplished some amazing feats by acquiring the proper knowledge. He has found that many things can be done cost-efficiently if you know what you're doing. He will definitely look into it. Sunday is drawing near again, and John knows that he needs every cent that he can get his fingers on. He decides to devote the rest of the week to a sermon that will make his TV congregation yearn to send him money.

John is dangerously close to sealing the fate of his soul.

CHAPTER FIVE
JUDGMENT DAY

John isolates himself for days while he constructs the perfect offensive against his fellow Americans. Adrenaline surges through his body as his mind pieces together the most incredible campaign in history. John second-guesses his commitment to the cause. The burden of guilt weighs heavy just thinking about the destruction that he is contemplating. For a moment, John even doubts that he is following the path of righteousness. He knows that he has to make a decision, the most important one of his life. He figures that it won't hurt to investigate his ideas.

$$\Omega$$

John has his plan to destroy the world all mapped out on a time line. He calls the operation Judgment Day, although it will probably take years to complete. The first step will be to acquire a biological or chemical weapon and a way to release it on every military base, government agency, and police station in the country, preferably all at the same time. John wants to eliminate any trained personnel who can oppose him with force. Second step is to clone an army that will sweep through the countryside finishing off any survivors and take control of all the military bases and their equipment. Third step will be to secure the country keeping everything operational and regrouping if necessary. During this time a religious cleansing process will begin. John will also be recruiting a new army. The rest of the time line will be finished as John proceeds from this point. Once he has the country's military resources, John figures that he will take the rest of the world by force, one country at a time.

Ω

John's plan is a good one and he knows that it will work, provided he can pull off the biological warfare and the clone army. All he has to do is recruit the right people with the knowledge to accomplish these tasks. John has to be extremely careful now. One word to the wrong person and John knows that he will be sitting in prison faster than he can shake a stick. John is making a profile on every person in the country with the knowledge and experience in the two fields. He is running into a lot of dead ends. John has read about a computer genius that has been sitting in jail for years. He has embezzled money from a number of large corporations and has served the time for the crime, but can't pay back the money that he has stolen. John makes a deal with the man to pay off his debt in return for hacking into secure sites for John.

John is already getting ahead of himself. Once the hacker is in Eden, John starts to get paranoid about strangers finding out about his plans and blowing the whistle. John needs some help from his family to keep an eye on these newcomers, but they don't know about his plans either. Frankly, John is worried about the same thing from his followers. John has trusted all of them with everything so far but a full-scale terrorist attack to take over the world is a different story. John knows that he has control of all the young runaways in Eden. It's the ones from his original congregation that he is worried about.

John picks his closest friend, who he has known since a few weeks after becoming a minister, to be the first one to hear his plan. If John can't trust his friend, then he can't trust anybody. John takes some time to step back and think of how far he is willing to go. He's walking the fine line between all or nothing. There are fifty or so acres of woods along the back side of Eden. John's friend has been asking to cut the timber for months. John has been too busy to look at the timber but decides to indulge his friend. It will give John the perfect opportunity to divulge his plan to his friend. John spills his guts, and he can tell by the look on his friend's face that he is not going to be on board. John's friend tells him that he is insane and needs to get help. He then tells John that he will never be able to succeed, and he will not let John ruin everything that they have built by trying.

John has spooked his friend, and he turns to head back towards town. John grabs a dead snag from the ground and smashes it over his buddy's head. The guy lay face down on the ground, semi conscience, with his head split open and bleeding. Things have quickly spun out of control. John tries to remain calm and regain his composure. He just stands there thinking the whole situation over. After about five minutes, John is snapped to attention when his buddy calls to him for help, not realizing that John has hit him. John stands straddling his friend's back. The wounded man struggles to look up at John out of the corner of his eye. John slowly leans over and says, "Judgment starts today." As his friend screams no, John lines up the branch and smashes it into exactly the same spot, crushing his skull. John calmly places the snag on the ground and slowly starts walking back to town. When he gets close enough to see Eden, he starts to run. He frantically runs through town begging for help. He explains, between his sobs, that a dead branch fell out of a tree and struck his buddy on the head. Of course, John gets lost in the woods and has trouble finding the accident site. By the time the doctor gets there the man is dead.

Ω

Everybody in Eden is trying to comfort John for the tragic loss of his dear friend. John is busy comforting his friend's wives. John is surprised that he feels no guilt what so ever. He figures that there must not be anything to feel guilty about, because he is doing God's work. John struggles through his friend's eulogy. Everybody thinks that he is having a hard time dealing with his friend's death. In all reality he can't concentrate because he is too busy thinking about his mission. John has to reprioritize his problems. His biggest hurdle might be his own people. He decides to keep as many people out of the loop as possible, but it will be hard with them living right on top of the project. John has enough young brainwashed people to do his bidding for now. He tells them that it will be a lot of hard work and total secrecy is a must, but

God and John will reward them in the new world. The computer hacker basically traded in one jail cell for another, but this time John is rewarding him for a job well done with a woman. This keeps the hacker very happy, and he puts anything John wants on the computer screen.

The hacker proves to be invaluable to John. He even guides John down easier paths than he was going to take. The hacker provides John with a government list of suspected terrorists living inside of the country. A couple of the names on the list are suspected of biological warfare. All John has to do is approach them. John picks the most qualified man, but he is afraid to be seen talking to the terrorist. If the man's name is on a list, the government has to be watching him. It takes John a couple of days to come up with a plan. He sends one of his most trusted young men to make contact with the terrorist. The terrorist lives in a huge apartment building, and the young operative manages to rent an apartment on the same floor as the terrorist. The two quickly become acquainted, and the terrorist is invited to the others apartment one evening to play cards and drink beer. John's operative wastes no time in soliciting the terrorist, in case they are being watched. He does not tell the terrorist that John is planning to take over the whole world, just his own country. The terrorist is informed that the government is watching him. If John can sneak him into Eden, the government will not be able to arrest him, but they have to act fast. All that and a wad of cash, and John has himself a biochemist that is more than happy to help.

Ω

John does not want to use a terrorist, but one man can be controlled. John figures that as long as he can get the terrorist into Eden, he can either imprison or kill the terrorist if things do not work out. John will not let any loose ends in the outside world. John and his young apprentice have the plan all worked out and ready to go when the terrorist agrees to go to Eden. The young man has all the supplies for him and the terrorist to disguise themselves as each other. They trade identities, apartments, and car keys and the terrorist has directions to drive straight to Eden early in the morning before daylight. The young man quickly walks to the terrorist's apartment around midnight and goes straight to bed. He wakes at the terrorist's normal time, gets into the terrorist's car and heads towards the terrorist's job, disguised as the terrorist. On the way he stops at a public restroom, walks inside and removes his disguise as fast as he can. He walks right back out and then enters a coffee shop across the street to watch the restroom. About a half hour later two men in suits rush into the restroom, then come back out and start searching up and down the street. The young man sneaks out the back of the coffee shop and calmly walks away. He is gripping a small pistol tucked in his pocket, ready to end his life if anybody recognizes him.

Ω

The terrorist was crossing the state line by first light. It will be dark again before he reaches Eden, which is what John has planned. John meets the terrorist on the outskirts of the property then sneaks him inside of Eden. The plan works perfectly. Nobody has a clue that there is a suspected terrorist in Eden, not even the people who live in the small community. John immediately begins construction on an underground laboratory complete with everything that the terrorist requested. The lab is built inside and underneath a warehouse. Nobody even knows anything is being built underground. John assigns a couple of his more intelligent youth to be the terrorist's assistants and also to keep an eye on the terrorist, which John does not trust. The young assistants are ordered to learn everything the terrorist knows about biological warfare while they all work on developing a weapon.

Ω

Meanwhile, John's hacker has found a scientist, named Dr. Janzen, who has spent his life developing a cloned army for the government. When Dr. Janzen's project was ready to be tested, the government shut him down and told him that it's unethical to clone a human being. He was given a piece of crap job cloning cattle to be eaten. Dr. Janzen agrees that it's unethical, but figures that it's more unethical to send men with families off to war to be killed for a cause that politicians feel is just. He wanted to genetically alter the clones not to feel emotions or think for themselves. They would be the perfect soldiers, and Dr. Janzen is spiteful towards the government for shutting him down. Of course, when John is soliciting Dr. Janzen, he leaves out his plans for overthrowing the government and killing most of the population. The scientist jumps at the chance to continue his work. He disappears from society and into Eden.

Ω

John puts Dr. Janzen to work right away. He builds another lab and assigns a whole team to the scientist to learn and to help. The first thing needed is a specimen to clone. John finds the most decorated soldier in the country and sends two women to find him. The soldier is a cold-hearted killer who will follow any order without a second thought. The women track the soldier down and, while he is on leave for the weekend, they follow him into a bar. A few hours later the women get a sample of his DNA in the back seat of their car in the parking lot. The two women rush the sample back to Eden, and the clone army is started.

Ω

Dr. Janzen and John are discussing altering the clones DNA, to basically make them mindless servants, and an idea pops into John's head. He thinks back to when he was a kid and dreamed of someday having the technology to make himself stronger and faster than anybody else. John asks Dr. Janzen if it's possible to improve the clone's physical prowess. Dr. Janzen tells John that it is possible, but he will have to find another specimen that has the features that he is looking for. John thinks for a while and then asks

100

him if he can combine animal DNA with human DNA. Dr. Janzen just laughs until he realizes that John is dead serious. John can see the fear in the scientist's eyes but can also tell that he wants to say something. Dr. Janzen knows that he should not say what he is thinking, but he does anyhow. He tells John that it would have to be DNA that is close to humans, like a chimpanzee. John is thinking out loud and says, "The countries best soldier with the strength and agility of an ape. Let's do it." Dr. Janzen quickly warns John that they will have to be careful screwing with nature like that. John tells the scientist, in a cocky tone, that he has been screwing with nature long before they met. Dr. Janzen gives John a puzzling look. John reluctantly leaves the awkward situation more determined than ever to create a mutant warrior.

John quickly buys a chimp, and the first clone is being grown. It's a long process, and John can't wait to see the outcome. If the experiment is a success, John wants to clone twenty at a time, maybe even more. He works on preparations for multiple clone growth as well as barracks to hide all the clones. Finally the experimental clone is done. It is a hideous looking creature. The clone is about six and a half feet tall but seems to have a slight hunch in its back. The clone has hair only where a normal man has hair, but it's long and thin, lying over irregular bulging muscles. It has rather large slightly deformed ears, a huge wrinkled forehead with large eye sockets, beady black eyes, and a large protruding chin. Dr. Janzen wants to destroy the clone and start again, but John stops him. The clone is scary looking, and fear is a powerful weapon.

They sneak the clone out to the woods to field-test it and John is very pleased with the results. It is a physically amazing creature that learns and follows simple orders to a tee. The clone will be a killing machine. John orders the mass production to start. After the next twenty are done, Dr. Janzen comes to his senses and refuses to do any more. He was blinded by his ambition. He finally realizes that his dream is to save lives with the clones, and John is planning to use them to kill millions. John tells Dr. Janzen that he will never leave Eden and, if he wants to live, he will continue his work. John has his people watching Dr. Janzen like a hawk and learning everything there is to know about cloning.

Ω

John puts the clones to work digging and building the underground lair. He builds an impressive labyrinth of tunnels and barracks right under Eden. When he is done the whole town is undermined. John is growing impatient with his terrorist and threatens to kill him if he does not produce. The whole time that John is orchestrating his sick and twisted plot, he is on TV every Sunday in a million homes preaching the word of God. Most of them are regularly sending John money, which is financially supporting his plot to kill them.

Finally the terrorist has something for John. It's a type of flesh-eating bacteria that can be passed on by touch. John wants an airborne agent and is not happy. He asks the terrorist how they are supposed to touch every soldier and cop in the country. The terrorist explains that all someone will need to do is touch one person from each military base and police station and they will spread it among themselves. A human body will carry the bacteria, while it incubates, for about six months before it does any damage. During that time it can be spread by direct contact or through any inanimate object for a few hours after the initial contact. There is no cure, but he did develop an immunization to prevent incubation. An immunized person probably will carry the bacteria for a month or so until it abandons the body. John still figures that it will be hard to make contact with everybody that needs to be infected. The terrorist comments that John's pretty young girls should be able to get any man in the country to touch them.

John does not want to admit that the terrorist is right, but he is. John orders him to get enough of the bacteria ready. John also tells him to get two thousand immunizations ready for all the people in Eden and all of the clone soldiers. John immediately shifts into overtime. He makes a huge map of the country and hangs it on the wall with every military base, government agency, and police station marked and numbered. John is organizing phase one of the attack, which will be executed six months before his army will be ready. It still is a lot of places to infect. John increases the clone production from twenty to fifty at a time and reserves ten of those spots to clone some girls to help carry out phase one. John picks out a dozen girls and has them cloned. John then teams them up in pairs and assigns targets to them. Each pair researches and stakes out each location to be sure of a quick and easy infection.

Everything is going as planned. Only now does John know for sure that Judgment Day is going to happen. For the first time he is getting nervous. John thinks about calling the whole thing off. His research has silently implicated him though. It will be hard to erase what has already happened. John realizes that every day his choice diminishes more and more. He reviews over every aspect of the plan time and time again until he decides that he can prepare no more. Then it occurs to John that he has an army, but no weapons. And if his clones have weapons, will they know how to use them. The clones can dig tunnels by hand like nobody's business, but can they fight. John will have to find a way to arm and train his army.

Ω

The hacker downloads some military tactics and training exercises while the terrorist hooks John up with some black market assault rifles. Acquiring enough rifles will be a long process. Only a small amount can be smuggled in at a time instead of the large amount that John ordered. John is also buying large quantities of machetes, axes, and hunting knives to be divvied up as secondary weapons. John studies the military tactics while he assigns some of his loyal followers to command and train the clones. Training is difficult on account of the fact that they have to stay hidden. One of the huge empty warehouses that hide an entrance to the underground bunkers becomes the training area. The clones learn to fight by sparring with each other. John figures that if they learn how to take down each other, then a human will be a piece of cake. John buys a surplus of pellet guns to teach the clones how to shoot. In no time at all the clones become expert marksmen that can pick off anything, anywhere in a split second. John's confidence is growing by the day.

Ω

John wants to execute phase one in the upcoming Spring, that way phase two can be launched in the fall going into winter. John plans to cut anybody left alive off from any other part of the country and keep the public immobilized. The country has gotten so soft that most survivors will have trouble surviving the winter. John will put the word out about Eden. He figures that many people will surrender to live in the new paradise. Spring is drawing near and John can see that his army is not going to be ready by the fall. John does not want to wait another full year though. It's hard to hide an army, and he knows that if he loses the element of surprise, it will be all over before it begins. After a couple of sleepless nights, John makes the call to launch phase one in three weeks and orders double production of clones. Even if clone production is doubled, John knows that he still will not have as many as he wants, but it will be close enough.

Ω

The first thing that needs done for phase one is to administer the vaccinations. Everybody involved in Judgment Day is being vaccinated when John realizes that he neglected something. How will he explain the shots that everybody else in Eden needs? He might be able to fool the majority of his people, but not his medical staff. The immunizations need to be administered at least two weeks before the bacteria is released. When John asks whether or not it can be put in the food, the terrorist explains that there will be no way to be positive that everyone will get the proper dose. One person's plate might contain more than another's or some might not eat the food that they put it in on that particular day. There is not enough of the vaccine ready to put it in multiple foods or on multiple days. The terrorist thinks that he can have enough to properly administer it in the food within the month. John is not willing to wait. Things are started and he is not going to stop the momentum. He just tells his biological team to do the best that they can with what they have.

One of the biological team members goes to see his buddy who works in the kitchen, and he asks which meal everybody seems to like the most. His buddy simply points to three big kettles of soup brewing on the stove. He races back to the lab and the team scrambles to divvy up the rest of the vaccine into the three kettles of soup. After dinner one of the team members goes back to the kitchen to see if all the soup is gone. Two kettles have a small amount in the bottom that isn't worth ladling out and the third kettle is half full. The terrorist warns John not to release the bacteria until he has enough time to make more of the vaccine just to be sure. John will not hear of it and is just going to take his chances. Those people are not crucial to the mission anyhow.

Ω

The day that phase one begins quickly rolls around. Early in the morning all the girls line up, and the bacteria is injected into their arms. John has outright bought a used car lot, which had just enough cars to supply the girls with transportation. The cars were all moved to a backfield in Eden, gassed up and ready to go. John has made multiple entrances to the highway past Eden through the fields so they will not draw attention with a parade of cars rolling through the middle of town. Many will use the treacherous back entrance and speed through the woods with an armed escort to scout ahead and eliminate anybody in their path. Each team knows exactly where they are going and exactly what they are going to do. John gives each team one thousand dollars in order to accomplish the task at all costs. The girls all jump into their cars and take off in every direction.

Ω

For two weeks, men all over the country are having experiences that they will talk about for the rest of their lives, which will last about six months. The girls have no trouble what so ever infecting all the targets. All of the men are more than happy to let the girls kiss and rub all over them. There is not a man approached that does not at least cop a feel. The girls have orders to return in two weeks. If they are not sure if they infected all of their targets, they are to be injected a second time and try again. In two weeks, all of the girls have returned with complete success in launching phase one. John decides to quarantine the girls for a few months due to the vaccination situation with Eden.

Ω

John has six months to prepare for phase two, and the pressure is on. He hounds the cloning team constantly to work faster. They have the capability to grow a hundred clones at a time now, and John has them working in a twenty-clone rotation. That way there are two units completed every week or so. Also the team is constantly working instead of working a while and waiting a long while. John knows he will lose some of his soldiers in the ensuing takeover but always figured that he would have plenty. Now that he sees that is not the case, he decides to try to protect his soldiers a little more. Now that the damage is done in phase one, John becomes less cautious about drawing attention to himself. He is ordering every piece of military equipment he can get hold of. He is mainly concerned with bulletproof vests and old helmets, but there just are not enough available to the public to outfit his army properly. He then turns to sports equipment. John buys anything that they can strap on themselves that might deflect a bullet.

All the equipment is laid out in a warehouse, and the clones are told to pick out equipment and modify it if necessary. John gets some of the handymen to help, and they are fastening sheet metal to anything that they can. Football and motorcycle helmets, which has to have the lining removed so they will fit over the clone's head, chest protectors, and any kind of pad John can think of. The handymen get quite creative and try to instill a bit of intimidation into their work. John notices all the trips to every hardware store for miles and the buying up of all the tin, screws, and pop rivets that they have. He is curious but also upset that his army's equipment is being pieced together and rigged up. Who will take him serious when his army looks like a bunch of poor kids playing football and hockey with newspapers and catalogs as protective equipment?

Ω

John is busy planning phase two. He has to decide how many soldiers to send to each location, and he does not have enough to comfortably cover every location. John is torn between under manning every location or skipping the less important locations. He decides to hit the military bases, government agencies, and bigger city law enforcement full force. He figures that the many small police stations and sheriff offices across the country will be easily dealt with if there is even any left alive. Once he captures the military bases and has the country's weapons and equipment, he will be unstoppable.

Ω

John's curiosity gets the better of him. He calls for an inspection of his troops in full battle gear. He is afraid of what he is going to see and prepares himself not to look disappointed. As he walks through the door, there is a warehouse full of the scariest-looking creatures he has ever laid eyes on. John's attitude changes, and he is quite pleased. People will run for the hills if they see what John is looking at coming towards them. John tells the handymen how pleased he is and asks them to outfit every soldier until they catch up to the cloning team. That will be their new job, armoring every new clone until John seizes the military bases. Then John tells them that he might even have them do their work to the updated vests and helmets.

Ω

Everybody involved in Judgment Day is working at a feverish pace. John is concerned about the quality of work being done, but the time is drawing near and John has no choice but to keep pushing. John is concerned about himself also. He is doing his best at keeping it together, but he is under tremendous stress. John keeps realizing that he has forgotten little, but crucial things like transportation for his army. He concentrated so much on getting his hands on military equipment and weapons that he did not think about how to get his army to the bases. They can't just walk there. John thinks about the cars that the girls used, but only four soldiers max will fit in most of the vehicles and there are nowhere near enough of them. Besides, that would look pretty pathetic and non-intimidating. John spends the next couple of weeks buying tractor-trailers and box trucks.

The trucks will work great for transportation, but it still takes a lot of them and that is too much to keep inconspicuous. John is finally drawing attention to himself and the mission. It does not take long for questions to be asked. John is so stressed out that he can't even come up with a story. He simply tells people that they will find out within the month. Eden's oblivious population is stunned by John being short with them and then just walking away, not answering their questions. They have never seen John like that before. It's now obvious that something major is about to happen. Things are past the point of no return and hopefully John's army will be moving as fast as the news.

Things are close enough now that John starts anticipating the first news of the bacteria. He is so nervous that he thinks he is getting an ulcer. All of a sudden John realizes that he has overlooked something else. There are probably thousands of military troops stationed all over the world. John feels like he has molten lead in his stomach and starts to panic. John is mad at himself for not thinking of them in the beginning. If he would have thought about them, he might not have even tried his plan. Regardless of any decision John will make now, the overseas troops will surely fly home to the rescue and John will have to fight them toe-to-toe. John is confident that his soldiers are as good as any, but he knows it will come down to fire power which he is short on. He will have to take the military bases before they can be reinforced.

Ω

John changes his plans again and will launch phase two as soon as he receives word that all the targets have been infected. He will not be able to wait for a handful more of clone units. Timing is more important than force. The lack of clone soldiers will not matter as long as John gets the jump on the military bases. John has his hacker get information about equipment and weapons on the bases and print operating manuals for all the soldiers to study while they wait. John figures there will be no time to organize and orientate at the bases before they will have to fight overseas troops. Without full use of military equipment, John will not be able to defeat the troops. They have to be ready.

Ω

It's a week before the six-month mark of phase one, and John gets some disturbing news. There is a major problem in the cloning lab. Two batches of clones have come out severely disfigured to the point where they are nothing but a lump of flesh. Nobody knows what the problem is or how many will turn out that way. The cloning team has already worked on the problem for a week, and it will be two more weeks until they find their mistake and start producing again. A full one hundred clone cycle is ruined. The incident puts John two months behind schedule. He is furious and if it were not for needing the cloning team so badly, he would have them all executed. John suspects Dr. Janzen of sabotage but can clearly see that the cloning team will still be lost without their lead scientist, which saves his life.

By now, John is about to have a nervous breakdown waiting for news of the bacteria. He decides to send all of the girls back to their targets to investigate. The girls no sooner leave until John hears a news report that a strange infectious disease has shown up in three cities across the country. John thinks God is helping him by delaying things a little so his cloning production can catch up. He relaxes a little and rallies his army to prepare for the launch of phase two. John is not hiding anything anymore. His army marches out of the warehouses with their armor glistening in the sunlight. The uninvolved people of Eden watch in horror and some even run for their lives. What they are seeing with their own eyes is too unbelievable to even comprehend. Even though John does not trust his people, he still feels loyal to them. He pulls a truck into the middle of town, crawls onto the roof and informs his people of his actions.

As John starts his speech, he notices some stragglers hobbling in and hunched over like they are in pain. He immediately realizes that it's the bacteria, and he starts to stutter and stammer around. By the time he is done talking, a few of his people are rolling around on the ground in pain begging for an antidote. The rest just look at John like he is a madman. John can feel his people's stares piercing right through him, and he can tell that they feel betrayed. As John looks into his congregation's eyes, he can hear them asking him why he is hurting them without any of them saying a word. John quickly returns to his army and tries to ignore what is happening in town. The bacteria eats away at organs and muscle tissue, and many of the infected people of Eden describe it like they are on fire from the inside out. By evening the sounds of agony fill the air. John feels the need to be with his people, but he can't face them. No matter where John goes, he can't get away from the screaming. The burden of guilt is getting heavier with every step as John walks around in the dark looking at his town in turmoil. His makeshift hospital is a madhouse as doctors and nurses try to ease the pain until the infected people die. John watches some of his closest friends die a horrible death.

Ω

John sits in his office crying about what he has done when he receives his first call from the girls. The girl reports that they drove right into the base and went anywhere they wanted unopposed. There are dead bodies lying all over the place. The only people they see alive are at the infirmary and pay no attention to them at all. A few more reports come in telling John the same thing. Then it hits John. The government is keeping the infections quiet, no doubt buying time until reinforcements arrive. John runs from his office to launce phase two, but he hesitates. He is still feeling guilty for what he has done. He's also scared that he will meet military reinforcements at the bases. John wishes that he can call it all off, but there is no turning back now. If he does not seize control of the country, he will be crucified. It will be a race for the country's strongholds, and John launches his fleet.

Ω

John commands his own division of soldiers that are going to the nation's capital to overthrow the politicians and the President. They will follow another division to the capital's closest military base and await word that all targets are in John's control. John will then attack the capital with his new equipment and weapons to overthrow the government. John purposely avoided the capital with the bacteria because he wants everyone who ran the country to know what is happening and that it's John who will be judging them. John has the surrender of the President all planned out in his head, and he will do it in dramatic fashion.

As John follows his soldiers the news of the bacteria can't be contained anymore. Reports are coming in all over the country warning people about a killer disease that has already killed millions. Officials are already estimating that half the country's population has already died. John's first sight of the bacteria's wrath is when his convoy has to drive around an abandoned car and a body lying in the middle of the road. John's guilt is slowly giving way to the promise of success. The more confirmation of minimal resistance that John receives, the braver he becomes. The closer they get to the military base, the more sign of the bacteria there is. There are bodies lying all over the place. Eventually John's trucks stop swerving for the bodies and just start running over them. When John gets to the military base the tractor and trailers smash through the gates and fences. The clone soldiers pour out of the trailers and shoot anyone who remotely looks like a threat. John is taking no prisoners. The most of the people who are killed, are shot in the back as they run for their lives. John quickly occupies the whole base with almost no resistance.

All of the military targets are taken with ease. There are a few survivors here and there who put up a fight, but all are quickly suppressed. John only loses about a dozen soldiers, and that is a lot better than what he expected. Every other target is taken except for a few cities that are in complete chaos from riots and looting since all of the police have been killed. John's soldiers can't even drive into the cities because the highways are log-jammed with abandoned and vandalized cars. John tells the units to just cover as many highways in and out of the city as they can and hold the city under siege. John figures he will just let them kill themselves. He will probably just bomb the cities off the map anyway. John tells the rest of his army to utilize as much fire power as they can and take defensive positions and prepare to be attacked.

John slows down a bit and takes some time to orientate his army with their new weapons. The clones follow directions to the tee and learn fast, but it will still take some time for them to become proficient with the weapons. The whole time John is looking over his shoulder waiting to get bombed at any second. He doubts that the military will destroy their own bases and weapons, but John has them at the point where they have no choice. John has an idea. He will race his division into the capital and claim that he has survivors being held as prisoners at the bases. This way his army will be protected from bombing. If reinforcements are on the way, John's only hope is to beat them to the capital. If he can do that, he should be able to buy his army enough time to become a deadly force.

Ω

John and ten of his unit commanders have taken flying lessons to get a jump on using military planes and helicopters. It will still take time to become aces and to be able to teach clones, but at least they have the basic principles of flight down pat. John knows any ground forces can be picked apart from the air, so he wants to control the skies as well as the ground. He temporarily plans on fighting sea battles from the air also and just hopes they will not lob missiles onto their own soil. John quickly takes to the air in a heavily armed helicopter. He heads towards the capital with a convoy of tanks and armored vehicles filled with cloned soldiers behind him. John needs some target practice and figures the government buildings of the capital will do just fine.

The whole time John keeps wondering where the overseas troops are. He begins to think they are in the capital waiting for him. John is scouting about a couple miles ahead of the convoy when he starts second-guessing his decision to spare the politicians from the bacteria. He gets nervous and falls back, circling the convoy. The President's military advisors have been trying to convince the President to call all troops home for weeks. The President refuses, explaining that he is not going to bring the troops home just to get sick and die until he knows what he is dealing with. If the country does come under attack and is overthrown, at least there will be a military force to retaliate.

Everybody in the capital city knows that all of the military bases are now occupied by an unfriendly force. When they hear that John is coming their way, everybody with a weapon begins circling the wagons to defend the city. Since every government bunker and hideout in the country is infected with the bacteria, there is nowhere to run to. The President orders his military advisors and Secret Service agents to flee the city. They all refuse with every intention of being killed on the spot to protect the President and their country. The President tells them that they have to go because they are the country's only hope. They have to gather up survivors and organize them to fight. He wants the military staff to assess the situation and collaborate with overseas troops to launch a counterstrike to regain control of the country. The President tells them, "Whoever these people are, they got the drop on us and we must pick a better fight." The President's loyal soldiers lower their heads and sneak out of the city.

Ω

When John gets in sight of the city and finds nothing but a police barricade, he knows that there is no military to oppose him. He gives orders to attack but do not harm any media coverage. He swoops down over the police cars and starts launching rockets into government buildings around the President as people run for their lives. John misses his first intended target, which is larger than the broad side of a barn. He is embarrassed, which makes him angry. He unleashes total destruction on the city below. Policeman and a small military guard open fire on John. John comes around and riddles them with machine gun fire. Two tanks lead the convoy side by side and they both fire into the police cars, blowing them thirty feet into the air in a giant fireball. Half of the defensive forces have already been killed, and the rest fall back desperately looking for cover. As John and the tanks finish off the rest of the buildings in range, he orders the clone soldiers out of the armored vehicles to finish off the police and guards on the ground. He commands his soldiers to conserve ammo and to show no mercy. John wants to make a point and wants the whole world to see. John could have easily done the job without harming any of his soldiers, but he is willing to sacrifice a few in order to scare the living hell out of everybody who is watching.

Ω

The mere site of the clone soldiers coming after them sends most of the defenders running. A handful stand their ground and open fire, killing two clones right away. The clones charge so fast that the defenders do not have a chance. It's all over in a matter of seconds. The clones are leaping and bounding over cars and fences that the men have to go around. The fleeing defenders are chased down and brutally and primitively killed. The sight looks like lions chasing down deer. The clones let the men scream for a few seconds before breaking their necks or chopping their heads off. People are so scared that they are running from the city without a clue as to where they are going, and they are not looking back. John lands his helicopter and storms the presidential office with his clones. There are two more men inside who launched a Hail Mary attack on John and his soldiers. They only get off one shot each before they are shredded with bullets. One of the bullets grazes John's arm, but he is on such a power trip that he does not even realize that he is bleeding. The clones smash through the presidential office doors, and John strolls in demanding the President's unconditional surrender.

John sends a couple of soldiers back outside to gather up a few news crews to cover the surrender. With cameras rolling, the President surrenders to John. John then addresses the nation explaining that he is the commander of God's army, and he will cleanse the world of sin. Everyone will be judged by John and, if they are saved, John will embrace them and they have nothing to worry about. Anybody who defies John will be sent to hell. Still fearing attack from troops abroad, John claims that he has thousands of prisoners being held at locations that his army holds, including Eden, which will become the new capital. He tells the cameras that everybody needs to go about their daily business and keep the country operational. Anybody who needs help can come to Eden if they accept God and are willing to live the way God intended.

John takes the President prisoner and loads him up into the helicopter to fly back to the base. John questions the President about the military stationed around the world and whether or not they will attack. The President, believing John about the prisoners, does not tell John that they are not coming in order to keep the prisoners safe, especially if there are any military personnel among them. John is pleased with the progress his army has made back at the base. He calms down a little. As he looks at his arm, he becomes a little rattled at how close he was to being killed. John had to be the one leading the President out of office after he surrendered, but he figures that will probably be the last time that he is on the front lines. All the bases are secure and everything is going as planned. John orders his division back to Eden, taking as much firepower as they can while he and the President flies in the helicopter. John lands his helicopter right in the middle of Eden and parades the President through the middle of town in shackles. John holds his head so high that he almost falls backwards. Once back at Eden, John feels at ease for the first time in quite a while. He locks the President in an underground bunker and begins planning his palace that he seen in his vision.

Ω

John can't help thinking about the President, locked away under his control. It occurs to John that the President is not the president anymore. John is the president. He is in control of every person in the country. Every acre now belongs to him. It's a power that John cannot manage. It's an aphrodisiac that he cannot resist. He fetches a young girl who helped spread the bacteria that has caught his eye. The girl is smitten with John's attention. He lavishes in the spoils of victory. John is unaware that his directives are already changing inside of his euphoric mind.

CHAPTER SIX
REFUGEES

Even though John told the nation to go about their daily business, most of the country is falling apart. Just about all of the major cities are in complete chaos, and people are running for their lives. Most of the people in the cities do not even know that the country has been overthrown or that they are under siege. The cities have already turned into their own little violent world. The rest of the country's turmoil, which the rest of the world is watching, is not even news inside of the Hell that used to be some of the most influential cultural centers of the world. Power grids are shutting down, people are running out of food and water, and winter is right around the corner. People have no choice but to become refugees and set out to try and find a better place. The peoples' boring and mechanical lives has been turned upside down into a life of scrounging for food and avoiding the violence that now occupies their streets. People start migrating from the cities like giant herds of caribou.

Ω

By this time, all of the clone units had been supplied with full military weapons and gear. When the refugees see the clone soldiers barricading the major highways in and out of the city, they think that the military is there to help them. People flock to the clones expecting help. All it takes is one nervous clone, in one city, to get spooked enough to open fire into the mob of refugees that is forming around them. A chain reaction slaughter reverberates around the city. Hundreds of innocent people are gunned down in a matter of seconds until the unit leaders get their soldiers under control. The surviving people flee back into the city only to try and find other ways out around the soldiers any way they can.

In the other cities the clone units are so encircled by people begging for help that many people start leaving the city between the units and there's nothing the soldiers can do about it. The clone units somehow become the ones under siege. There are thousands of people becoming unaccounted for and out of John's control every day. Things are quickly spiraling out of control, and a huge unforeseen roadblock is developing in John's path to glory. John is very angry and has to leave Eden to try and gain control of the situation. He needs the people to stay put and keep everything operational until he has time to deal with them. John's plans for the population have already changed. Instead of killing most of the population off, John figures why not have them serve him. John's directive is turning from leading the people to live as God's servants, to becoming the dictator of a very prosperous country, still all in the name of God of course.

John orders the masses of refugees back into the cities and to live their lives as they always have. He is informed that the inner cities are war zones. Gangs are having their own little wars going on for control of the cities. They struggle for control of anything valuable for survival, each trying to get the upper hand on the other. For someone who had just planned and executed the takeover of the world's most powerful country, a bunch of hoodlums trying to get a piece of the action is a slap in John's face. His first instinct is to use the cities as target practice for his new air force. But he would still have hundreds of thousands of refugees to take care of. He decides to split his forces and send half to eliminate the gangs with extreme prejudice and the other half would tend to the refugees.

John figured that his clone soldiers would make short work of the riff raff gangsters. He quickly sends them off on foot, zigzagging through the wreckage on the street. When it came to the refugees, nobody has a clue how to deal with them. Eventually, John thinks of a solution. He spends the next several weeks traveling back and forth between the cities organizing and setting up a system to evaluate each refugee. After each refugee is evaluated, they are placed in one of two groups. Any family who would be an asset in John's ideal society is in one group, and all others who would be a burden in John's eyes are placed in the other group. John set up shelters in nearby buildings at each location keeping both groups separated. Once inside the shelters, all of the children and teenagers in the burden groups are taken from their families and shipped to Eden. John figured that the children would be perfect to mold into his minions. Originally, John planned to execute any kids that were unruly and uncooperative. After much thought about coming under heavy criticism for killing kids, he decides to sterilize the problem teens instead. It's a less harsh solution, and the uncooperative attitudes would eventually die out.

Ω

John also has to feed these people as well as his soldiers. Dealing with the refugees is taking more and more manpower and more of John's time. Every clone unit coming off the line is sent to the cities instead of strategic locations where they are desperately needed. John's trucks are constantly hauling soldiers and food to the cities and hauling children back to Eden. All of this is a major distraction to John's plan to take over the world. Once John falls behind schedule it's like a trap in which he can't recover from. The more off schedule he becomes, the more frustrated he becomes. John starts to realize that running the country is going to be more difficult than taking it over.

Food and water around the cities is starting to get scarce, as well as the fuel needed for trucking. John needs access into the cities and the clones are having trouble securing them. The clone soldiers are severely out-numbered and walking into ambush after ambush. The gangs are so spread out over the city that no matter where the soldiers go, they are constantly being shot at from windows in buildings all around them. While securing one building, the clones are under heavy fire from the next building, only to be under fire while securing the next building from the one that they had just secured. The clones are just going in circles and getting nothing accomplished while they are slowly being picked off one by one. John keeps sending more and more soldiers into the cities. It's an embarrassment to John that his army can't defeat a bunch of thugs that are barely even armed without destroying the city with bombs.

Ω

John is constantly giving sermons to the hoards of refugees about how the world was under Satan's influence and God had commanded him to wipe out sin and start over. He tells people that if they are saved they had nothing to worry about, but God will punish those who are not. John makes sure that all TV and radio stations stayed operational and broadcasting his sermons to the whole country. He commands people to go to work and live as they did before. It is the same country, just under new leadership. It must stay operational or God will punish them all. Word is already spreading throughout the country about the massacre of all the innocent refugees. The brutal takeover of the capital has been broadcasting from the beginning. Most of the people, except those in desperate need of help, are prepared to avoid John and his army at all costs.

Ω

John is forced to change his plan of attack for the cities. As much as he wants the gang members dead, he needs supplies more. He decides to have the clones inside the cities scout out supplies, secure them, and then stay with them until other units opened up travel lanes to haul the supplies out to the refugee camps. John will just continue to hold the cities under siege and let the gangs either kill each other off or starve to death. This plan is working better for the units that are fighting the gangs, but opening highways needs even more soldiers and equipment. The clones just are not being produced fast enough. John starts to pull in other soldiers from other units across the country to do the work.

Ω

All of the reinforcements are starting to make progress with the cities but left every other location that John held undermanned. Soon supplies start to arrive at the refugee camps and not a day too soon. All of the people are starving as well as John's soldiers. By the time the clones fill their veracious appetites there is not much food left for the refugees. It's not long until there is a problem with the supply convoy. The gangs quickly figure out what is going on and start beating the soldiers to the supplies. The gangs then hide the supplies in stashes throughout the city. It's back to a building-by-building search. This time the soldiers have armored artillery, which escort the trucks, to assist them. Every time the artillery is called into action to help secure supplies, the trucks are left alone and quickly disabled. John is losing equipment and soldiers fighting for small cashes of food, most of which is not even making it past the fighting soldiers mouths.

John is at the end of his rope with frustration and anger. He can't believe that he managed to overthrow the government but cannot control the citizens. John has always planned to kill the refugees that are of no value to him, but he wants to do it when nobody will see it. He decides to call in an air strike on the buildings housing the refugees marked for death in order to ease the strain on food and water. The hovering helicopters draw everybody's attention. The unwanted refugees watch as rockets are fired right into them. People are jumping out of windows on fire and crawling out of smoldering rubble missing arms and legs, as the people that John wants alive watch in horror from the neighboring buildings. Many people run for their lives thinking that they are next. The soldiers take target practice on any fleeing refugee as well as finishing off any mangled survivors. This goes on the whole way around every city under siege until every unwanted refugee is killed.

Ω

Many refugees escape and head into the countryside. It does not take long for their horror stories to start circulating around the country. People are warning each other that John is killing everybody no matter what their religious convictions are. If don't kill you, you will just starve to death in his camps. A news reporter also caught one of the brutal bombings on film, and it's broadcasting all over the country. John becomes furious when he finds out about the broadcast. John needs the TV and radio broadcasts to communicate with the citizens in order to make his job easier. This footage makes it much harder. As if he didn't have enough to do, now he has to censor everything being broadcasted. The reporter loses his head as a warning to the rest of the reporters.

Things are at a stand-still around the country and John can't get anything accomplished. Hundreds of thousands of refugees and soldiers are starving. The soldiers are stretched too thin to do anything effectively. John calls all of the units in the cities back to the siege lines to regroup and start sweeping across the country side away from the cities. John hates to give in to the gangs, but he has no choice. The gangs are crippling John's operation with time. John figures that his army will do better in the urban sprawl and rural areas of the country that are still functioning. John tapes a message to all of the citizens, which is added on to his regularly aired sermons. The message tells people that God's army is coming and everybody needs to embrace and support the army. The more cooperation and the less resistance there is, the quicker they will all be living in a paradise free from sin.

There is a lot of territory to cover, and John still does not have enough soldiers. The gangs are still costing John time. Every soldier coming out of Eden is replacing one that has been killed or detained in a refugee camp, which should not have even happened. It's almost spring, and John should have a full-sized army by now. There are barely any more soldiers now than when he started, and a large number of them are on work details babysitting refugees or looking for food. All of the military bases and the areas around them are like ghost towns. There is nothing at all for John's soldiers to do but stand guard over empty real estate. John makes the decision to cut his forces, which were guarding the bases, in half and send the soldiers to join the units that are sweeping the countryside. This is a risky move which leaves the military bases severely under-manned. John needs the soldiers to make some kind of progress. Once he has control over the rest of the country, he will restock the bases with soldiers.

John figures that as long as he holds the President and has completely broken the chain of command, there will be no impending attack from over-seas troops. John does not know about the President's military advisors who had escaped the capital though. They are watching the bases and trying to get organized. Time is of the essence and John wants to push through the country quickly. He sends his units out, lightly armed, in every direction with a heavy artillery unit close by for support. John's army quickly moves through the urban sprawl around the country with minimal resistance and supplies are starting to roll in. People are sitting around praying and waiting for God to judge them, or packing up and staying as far away from John and his army as possible. Although the farther the army travels, the more people they find barricaded in their homes ready to defend their families and property. Anybody who tries to fight the clone soldiers is killed, their houses are looted, and their bodies are burnt inside of their houses. The same fate awaits anybody who is not essential to the operation of the country, just like at the refugee camps.

Ω

Overlooking all of the rural law enforcement offices across the country will prove to be a big mistake on John's part. That decision left a lot of trained people between John's army and Eden with easy access to a lot of fairly heavy firepower. In the rural parts of the country, just about every other house has a couple of high-powered hunting rifles or at least a shotgun. There is also plenty of ammunition available. Every town with a police station or a sheriff's office has been recruiting locals ever since the government fell. They are prepared to defend their towns, and every one of them knows how to shoot. John's soldiers start to encounter some of these well-armed towns, which catch John and his soldiers by surprise.

John's army is pushing hoards of people ahead like a giant cattle drive. John is herding everybody from the borders of the country towards the center, which will end up being close to Eden. Once everybody meets somewhere in the middle, John can deal with the population without having to chase them around. After John's religious cleansing, his personal little town will be the biggest and most powerful city in the country, and eventually the world. With more and more people running from the army, things are too easy for the soldiers and they all become over confident and sloppy. The first few clone units that stroll into one of the ambush towns are completely wiped out. The clone soldiers are shredded by deadly aimed rifle bullets. They have no armored vehicles, so they have no protection once their personnel carriers catch fire from being riddled with bullets. The desperate clones run for cover between the houses. They usually meet head-on with a rifle or shotgun blast from a window or shrub, which takes them right of their feet. It's a wake-up call to John's army, and every soldier becomes more cautious. The whole operation slows down even more. Still more and more reports come in from around the country that units are finding themselves pinned down by snipers all around them.

Ω

The disabled units leave holes in the line, which will leave too much unsecured territory. The whole line has to be halted until reinforcements arrive to crush the spots of resistance. John is unwilling to play cat and mouse with anybody else. He orders the bombing of any town that assaults his army. The towns are shelled by artillery or bombed from the air until the sharpshooters surrender. The men are trying to protect whatever is being blown off the face of the earth behind them. It doesn't take long for them to surrender. As soon as they do, they are killed. The town is looted and burnt. John uses these towns as examples of what will happen if anyone else defies him. John will not tolerate anyone who does not comply with his wishes. The lines are moving again and pushing towards Eden. There are even more people running from John now.

Ω

John is growing tired of trying to be in twenty different places at the same time. He takes a map of the country and draws two lines in a cross dividing the country into four equal parts. He chooses three of his most trusted and competent unit leaders and puts them each in charge of a quadrant. Each one will su-pervise operations in their quadrant while sweeping towards Eden. Once in Eden, John will take back all control, and he can handle everything from one loca-tion. Each quadrant still encounters spotty resistance, but the rebels are no match for John's tanks and air-craft now that operations are a little more organized. Even though the small bands of rebel fighters are doing nothing more than killing a few of John's sol-diers at a time, they are buying desperately needed time and a major diversion.

Ω

When the presidential staff escaped the capital, they devised a plan. The high-ranking military personnel stake out the military bases and coordinate an attack with overseas forces. The rest dispersed into the countryside and are trying to organize a militia to draw John's army away from strategic locations. They also plan to do as much damage as they can to John's army. Each man headed out into a different part of the country to recruit a militia. One of the President's Secret Service agents, named Jake Riley, has been trying to recruit men in John's quadrant for months, with little success. Most of the men are more than willing to fight but do not want to leave their families unprotected to do it. Many men stay to defend their homes, and most are now dead.

Jake has been recruiting up and down the country-side just ahead of John's sweeping army. Whenever the refugees start moving through, Jake knows that it is time to move on. Things are bad in the areas that are in John's immediate path. The people are scared.

Friendly communities quickly became frantic, very unfriendly, and unwilling to help anybody. It's almost impossible to get food, water, or fuel. Most of the refugees are on foot by now and in desperate need of help to stay ahead of John's army. With the biggest part of the population all heading to the center of the country, things are starting to get quite congested. People who do have supplies are hoarding the surplus for themselves. Desperate refugees start to take what they need. The people who do have supplies are willing to kill to keep them. Society starts to break down, and blood begins to spill out onto the streets before John even gets there.

Ω

Locals are not very receptive to strangers, which is seriously hindering Jake's recruiting abilities. Jake is getting run off more and more. People do not want John blowing up their towns and do not want to leave their families alone in John's path to make a stand somewhere on up the road. Jake realizes that he needs to get farther ahead of John. He needs more open ground to fight. He needs to recruit men who can retreat to their families. John has to cross the Appalachian Mountains to reach Eden, and Jake figures that is the best place to make a stand. Jake is a smooth city boy, but he was born and raised deep in the mountains. He left as soon as he was able and vowed to never return. Jake grew up poor and part of a social structure unlike any in the whole world, and he hated it. Everybody in his home county worked as a construction worker who was never home for weeks at a time, a farmer or a logger. Jake refused to fall into the rut that trapped all of his family before him. But he knows the people, he knows the woods, and he knows that is the only place he stands a chance against John. Jake has managed to recruit about a dozen men, and they set out for the mountains about seventy miles away.

Ω

It's slow going for the militia unit. Everywhere they go, locals have roads blocked in an attempt to keep John out. After a long day of looking at maps and zigzagging back and forth on back roads, Jake and his men's vehicles finally run out of gas. A vehicle is practically worthless anyway, and they set out on foot. The whole trip Jake has been studying maps looking for the best places to set up ambushes. All of the roads begin bottle necking down into the limited number of roads that cross the mountains. Jake decides to cover as many roads crossing the first mountain as he can and make his stand. He is still recruiting the whole way and has managed to pick up a couple more men as well as a couple of rides here and there.

Jake finally reaches the mountains and begins patrolling up and down the range accessing the situation. Jake and his men receive a little better reception at the edge of the mountains, but not much better. It's a little easier to recruit men and gather much needed supplies. Jake begins to stop every refugee heading over the mountains and shares a little food. He tells them to spread the word that a militia is making a stand, and any man that is willing to fight would be greatly appreciated. The refugees are still snubbed by many people. Most good Christians believe that God is destroying the world, and anybody that is running from it must belong in Hell. They keep as much distance as possible between them and the refugees, let alone help them. Just about everybody, even Jake, has a thought in the back of their mind of whether or not all of it is God's will. Jake reluctantly does not believe in the existence of God, but how could anyone else completely upset the country and strike down the entire military before anybody knew what was going on.

Ω

It's not long until men start coming down out of the mountains ready to fight. They are all anxious to stop John from reaching their homes. Jake is trying to get organized and establish a tactical plan. His militia is growing, but he knows that he will need to split his forces enough to cover at least a dozen roads that cross the first mountain. Jake is under more pressure now than he has been in his entire life. He wonders if he can handle it. He feels like going up into the mountains and sneaking right out of the country. Jake is not at all afraid to fight. He is afraid of getting everybody else killed and failing his mission in which millions of innocent people are unknowingly depending on him to accomplish. He can tell that his men trust him and are relying on him to lead them into battle. Jake knows that he has to pull through and not let his men down, who will fight with or without him to protect their families.

Jake decides that he needs a central headquarters where everything can be coordinated from. Even the simplest things that he took for granted before, like electricity, would be a blessing. He needs to make contact with his comrades that are attempting to do the same thing as him. He sits down with his map, which he has been plotting John's progress on, and picks out the best road to meet John head-on. As soon as he picks out the road, he remembers a small farm. The farm is about a mile off the main road nestled against the mountain. It would be perfect for his headquarters. Jake immediately heads for the farm. When he gets there he is abruptly meet by a young man, with a rifle in hand, telling Jake to go back out the way that he came in.

Jake is getting used to that kind of reception. He turns and starts walking back out the lane. His disappointment pushes him to try harder. He sits down his rifle against a tree along the rutty overgrown lane and asks the man if they can just talk. The man simply nods his head and meets Jake halfway. Jake holds out his hand and introduces himself. The man reluctantly shakes Jake's hand and says, "I'm Nate and there is another rifle in the house with the crosshairs on your chest." Jake gives a nervous little laugh as he explains who he is, what he was ordered to do, and what his plan is. Jake asks if he could use the farm, and Nate abruptly answers, "Absolutely not". After a short pause of dead silence, Nate goes on to explain in a more sincere tone that he has a family to take care of. Jake tries to reason that John himself, along with his mutant soldiers, will come right down the road destroying everything in his path, including Nate and his family. Nate tells Jake that nobody will think that there is anything down his lane. If they do come, all he has to do is take his family up on the mountain and hide until John passes through, then return to their home. Jake can tell that Nate is prepared with a plan and can't be convinced otherwise. Jake can't afford to waste any time, so he wishes Nate good luck and heads back out the lane.

As Jake walks back to the highway he convinces himself that his second choice for a headquarters might be a better location anyhow. It's an old abandoned hotel at the top of the mountain on the same road. It would not be as comfortable as the farm, but it's the high ground and there is a lookout where John can be seen coming for miles. Jake hustles everybody up the mountain to the old hotel. They fortify the location the best that they can. As Jake looks out across the valley, he is over come by an uneasy feeling knowing that he made a choice to make a stand there. Planning to do something is a lot easier than actually doing it. He can no longer run from John.

Ω

There are more people coming out of the mountains every day to fight John's army. With the people come much-needed supplies and vehicles, which will come in handy, moving up and down the mountainside. Jake is set up as good as he can be with the arrival of generators, more weapons and ammo, food and even chainsaws to cut firewood. Even though winter is turning into spring it still is plenty cold. Jake watches some men cut firewood down across a trail, and it gives him an idea. They could cut trees down across the roads to stop John's tanks and then attack while the clones are clearing the roads. If Jake and his men could attack on all of the roads at about the same time, they could do some serious damage to John's army before the clones even realize that it's a trap.

Ω

Jake finally makes contact with one of his buddies who is fighting John's army in the southern part of the country. John's army is held up down there mostly due to millions of starving refugees. John is using winter as a weapon, but he did not foresee everybody migrating to warmer climates. There are three enemies on the southern front. It's North against South all over again as millions of refugees from the north infiltrate southern lands anywhere they can squeeze in. The refugees are so desperate for food and a place to blend in that they are like zombies, relentlessly searching and more than willing to kill for it. Southern hospitality is murdered. Nobody knows who they are fighting from one day to the next. The only way that Jake's buddy can engage the clones is to blend in with the refugees, fight through the crowds, and open fire on the clones at point blank range. That usually ends up in a lot of innocent people being gunned down or a riot. Anticipation and mass confusion has everybody on the edge. It's not even safe to take your eyes off of your shoes.

Ω

West of Eden there is a bigger more rugged mountain range where the militia has John's army stopped dead. It's still well into winter in those mountains, and the militia is trapped. They have stopped the clones, but figure that they will freeze or starve to death while the clones wait for the spring thaw. Hundreds of thousands of refugees flee into the mountains leaving everything behind for the clones. Most never make it out of the mountains while the clones feast on their food and enjoy their homes. Nobody has heard anything at all from the military. The military has surrounded the entire country, but no one inside the country thinks that a rescue is coming.

Jake decides not to tell his men about the bleak situation that the whole country is in. He lies to them and tells them that everywhere else John's army is being defeated, and now it's their turn. The men cheer and are ready to lay down their lives right then and there. Visitors show up from the valley below that John is about to roll through. They demand that Jake and his men move on. They want John to move on through as quickly as possible. If there is conflict, they will be the ones who will suffer the most. Jake tells them that they are right and that he is sorry but no matter where he goes, people will feel the same. The mountainside is the best place to make a stand. Before Jake can defuse the situation, guns are drawn in a dangerous standoff. Both sides are yelling profanities and calling each other hillbillies and flatlanders. The visitors know that if one shot sounds off, they will all be dead so they lower their guns and leave.

A preacher from a big fancy church down in town stays and starts giving a sermon as he walks through the men. He tells the men that they are all

Satan's minions and do not even realize it. He preaches to the men that they have all heard the prophecy all of their lives and it is finally here. He asks the men why they do not believe it. The preacher yells out, "God is coming and if you strike the hand of God, you will be sent to Hell." As the preacher turns around to walk back through the men, Jake stops him dead in his tracks with a pistol to his forehead. Jake tells the preacher that he had better leave while he has the chance. As the preacher walks away he shouts into the air, "Forgive them Lord for they know not what they do."

Jake looks at his men knowing full well that the preacher just threw gasoline on the small flame of doubt in the back of everybody's mind. The preacher may have just done more damage to the men's chances than the clones can ever inflict. Moral has just dropped to an all-time low in about thirty seconds. Jake tries to rally the men again, but he is just not the speaker that the preacher is. Jake figures that the best thing to do is to keep the men so busy that they do not have time to think about it. He sends all of them to check and recheck their ambush locations. Jake fells guilty about lying and manipulating his men. He sends a few men out to shoot some deer and a few to get some booze. Evening drapes across the mountain and they eat a huge feast, which helps raise the men's spirits.

Ω

Jake is awakened the next morning by the sound of a helicopter. It's John, patrolling out ahead of his units. Everybody scrambles to hide anything that would give away the element of surprise. Once everything is as inconspicuous as possible at the hotel, they all head out to their locations to lay in wait for John's army. The men do not block the roads yet because John is still flushing people out of their homes like rabbits. People who had decided to take their chances with John are quickly changing their minds when they hear the screams and gunshots coming from their neighbor's homes.

Ω

The men lay in wait for two days until John's army reaches the foot of the mountain. John is beaming with confidence, but something about the mountain has him spooked. He decides to hold up for a day or so to scout out the mountain before he sends his army blindly up over. John had spied Nate's farm nestled in the woods from his helicopter and also thought that it would be a comfy place to set up for awhile. He halts all of his units at the base of the mountain and sends a unit in to check out Nate's farm. Time to think about what is about to happen is the one thing that Jake and his men do not need.

Ω

Nate has been watching the clones and when they stop near his lane he is still confident that they will not find his place, but he is taking no chances. He is completely prepared to escape into the mountain. He gathers his family and hurries off through a large field and up the ridge. They have a four-wheeler to ride through the field but hide it in the brush at the edge. Nate does not want any clones tracking them by a four-wheeler trail. He is about five hundred yards away from his house in thick cover and can see his house plain as day. They decide to wait there and watch to see if the clones show up. If the clones do find the farm, Nate and his family can easily continue on up the mountain unnoticed.

Nate, his pretty wife, and their two-year-old daughter nestle down in the brush and watch their house through binoculars. They're not there but five minutes when the two-year-old freaks out because they forgot her kitty. They all feel like the pet is part of their family but more importantly the little girl will not be quiet without her pet. Nate jumps up to go and get the cat. His wife stops him and demands that she go. She explains to Nate that if something should separate them, he can take better care of their daughter in that particular situation. Nate reluctantly agrees. He gives her a walkie-talkie and a shotgun, and tells her that he will watch for clones and should be able to see them early enough for her to get away. Before she leaves, she makes Nate promise to take their daughter and leave if something happens instead of trying to save her.

Nate nervously watches his wife speed down through the field and into their house as he scans the woods for clones. Minutes seem like hours until she finally comes out with the cat. She jumps on the four-wheeler and takes off up along the side of the house. She races past the corner of the house, and a huge hairy arm reaches out and clothes lines her right off the ATV. Nate jumps straight in the air to his feet, practically hyperventilating. His wife lay flat on her back with the wind knocked out of her as a clone walks around the corner of the house. The clone jerks her to her feet as more clones start to appear at the edge of the woods. Nate frantically wonders how he did not see them coming. As the clone holding her orders the rest to search the house and barn, she pulls out her walkie-talkie and screams for Nate to run. The clone knocks the walkie-talkie out of her hand, grabs her around the waist with its arm, and begins to pull her to the front porch. She resists, letting herself go limp while she kicks and thrashes around.

Nate panics and starts frantically pacing back and forth yelling, "Stupid cat, I can't believe I left her go back for a stupid cat." The sight of Nate coming unglued made his daughter cry. Nate crouches down to comfort her and to make her be quiet. The little girl calms down, and Nate throws his binoculars back up to watch. While the clone is dragging Nate's wife, its hand slips up under her coat and lands right on her breast. The clone stops and just stands there, not moving a muscle. The clone drops her on her back, kneels down beside her and starts to unzip her coat. She flings her leg up and kicks the clone in the face, knocking it backwards. She jumps up and runs for the shotgun on the ATV. The clone quickly catches her and smacks her up alongside the head. She tumbles to the ground with a thud. She lay there dazed while the clone rips her clothes off and rapes her.

Ω

Nate had his rifle aimed at the clone as soon as it began ripping his wife's clothes off. He is shaking so bad that he can barely keep the clone in the scope.

He knows that his 30-30 will never reach that far. If it did, he could just as easy hit his wife as the clone. The shot would also give up him and his daughter's position. Nate is struggling to contain his emotions as he frantically tries to think of what to do. Everything is happening so quickly. He knows that he has to do something fast. He grabs his daughter and takes off along the edge of the brush to get a closer shot. The thought of the clones getting a hold of his daughter pops into his head and stops him dead in his tracks. He races back to his gear, puts his daughter down and tells her to stay there and hide no matter what until he gets back. Nate only gets half as far this time until he thinks about his little girl scared and alone and probably not surviving the night if he does not make it back. He has no choice but to helplessly watch as his wife is violated.

$$\Omega$$

Finally the clone finishes and it goes into the house. Nate's wife rolls over to her hands and knees and starts crawling towards the woods. Nate's heart is ripped out over what had just happened, but at least she is alive. And it looks like she is going to be able to just sneak away. Nate anxiously plans her rescue. If she can just make it to the edge of the brush. As Nate gathers up his daughter again, he notices another clone walking up and standing in front of his wife. She hunkers down into a ball, covering her head with her hands. One by one, more clones show up until there are five of them circled around her. Nate is seriously freaking out. He frantically paces as he babbles out loud. He is desperate to stumble onto a solution to save his wife. He cannot let his wife get gang-raped. He figures that he can take out the clones, or at least create enough of a diversion that his wife can get away. Nate turns to tell his daughter to stay put. But one look into that sad, scared little face and he knows that he can never leave her. Nate has to make an impossible decision. He sits there with tears in his eyes while he watches every last clone rape his wife.

Ω

The clones all leave and Nate watches his naked wife, waiting for her to get up and start crawling towards the woods again. She is not moving at all. Nate notices a large pool of blood underneath her. Deep down Nate knows that she is dead, but he can't give up hope or leave her that way. He watches her for a couple of hours, begging for her to move, until he knows that he has to leave her. There is only about an hour of daylight left for Nate to get his daughter to the campsite that is ready and waiting for them. His daughter is cold, hungry and very upset. Nate knows that he has to hold it together for her. They reach the shelter that Nate had prepared, and he feeds and holds his daughter all night while she sleeps. Nate is crushed and guilt starts to consume his heart. He gently rocks his daughter back and forth as he whispers for forgiveness into the pitch-black night.

Nate gets no sleep at all and holds his daughter until she wakes in the morning. He can feel that he is going to lose it. He sits her down to play in a pile of rocks while he walks about fifty feet away to quietly deal with his emotions. Nate is crouched down with his back towards his daughter, crying, when he hears her scream. Nate wheels around to see a five hundred pound black bear dragging his daughter off by her leg. Nate throws up his rifle and instantly puts the crosshairs on the bear. Just as he is squeezing the trigger, his daughter flops up into the scope. Nate hesitates the shot for fear of hitting his little girl instead of the bear. He gets back on the bear just as it disappears into the mountain laurel.

Nate charges after the bear, jumping right through the brush that it disappeared into. He clears the brush and lands on his feet with his rifle to his shoulder, only to catch a glimpse of the bear disappearing into the brush again. He keeps racing towards his daughter's screams. He sees the bear a couple more times but just does not have a chance to get a shot off. Nate is zipping across the top of the rubble rock like he is floating through the air, but still the bear is faster. The little girl's screams stop. Nate can't see the bear anywhere. He continues on in the direction that he was heading until he reaches a long slope and can't see the bear. Nate is amazingly level headed considering what is going on, until he realizes that he has lost track of his daughter. As panic quickly starts to take over his mind, he races back to the point that he last saw the bear. He begins frantically searching in every direction as he keeps asking himself why he did not take that first shot.

Nate pours every once of energy he has into every stride as he frantically searches hundreds of acres of forest. He screams "no" about a hundred times in shear desperation to save his daughter. Nate finally collapses in complete exhaustion. He is bloody and bruised from falling in the rocks and brush.

The only pain that he feels is the intense pressure in his chest that feels like he is going to explode. The full weight of what has happened starts to set in, and he has a complete emotional breakdown. Nate lay on the ground screaming at the top of his lungs until he thinks about what is happening to his little girl at this very moment. An amazing burst of adrenaline explodes him to his feet. He is not going to give up. He cannot let this happen. He thinks that if he keeps pushing the bear, it might drop his daughter. He searches for several more hours maintaining a feverous pace. Nate holds on to the hope that his daughter might be laying somewhere unconscious. He just has to find her. That glimmer of hope keeps him going all day and well into the night until he collapses again and passes out.

$$\Omega$$

Nate wakes early in the morning to a light frost. He sits there for a couple of minutes, in a daze, coming to grips with the fact that his daughter definitely did not survive the night. Nate already has abandoned his wife's body, but he is not leaving the mountainside without his daughter. He gathers himself up and continues his search. Nate searches almost a week all over that mountain and does not find one sign of his daughter. He is physically and emotionally wiped out and heartbroken beyond belief. He can't take the pain anymore. He sticks his pistol into his mouth and slowly cocks the hammer. Nate tries to put pleasant memories of his family into his mind for the last moments of his life. Every time he envisions his family happy, John and his clones enter his mind.

Nate's excruciating sadness starts turning into anger like he has never felt before. Nate knows that his hatred for John and the clones will consume him until his last breath. He figures that if he is going to kill himself, he will let the clones do it. Nate will take as many clones with him as he can.

CHAPTER SEVEN
THE RESISTANCE

The past week has been nothing but problems for John. He can't make contact with anybody at Eden, and a deployment of clone soldiers never arrived at their destinations. The clones are desperately needed in every quadrant of the country. John's soldiers are coming under heavy attack from militia and refugees driven by starvation. John has been trying to talk his quadrant commanders through their situations all week. They are all in way over their heads and losing more and more soldiers every day. After much thought, John decides that clone production is the most pressing threat. He decides to fly to Eden and find out what is going on first thing in the morning.

Ω

Jake's men, that are stationed along the road in their ambush positions, are about to have nervous breakdowns by now. A week is way too much time to think and worry about their mission. The possibility that John is doing God's will, weighs heavily on everybody's mind. Every day the men doubt themselves more and more. There are even a couple of men who have deserted already. Jake can't take the pressure anymore either. He sends word out to all of the men

150

to sneak down to the clone camps after dark and see what is going on. Jake tells his men that if they get the drop on the clones and can successfully wipe at least half of them out, to do so. Jake also desperately needs every man. Realizing that he can lose a good many men by foolishly attacking, he stresses to his men not to get killed. Jake's orders are to only engage if the assault is a guaranteed success. He tells his men not to risk the lives of a dozen men for the chance to kill a couple of clones and to be patient and wait for a better opportunity if necessary.

Jake is confident that John himself is at Nate's farm. He rendezvous with the men on the highway above the farm. At dusk they sneak down through the woods to the edge of the fields to observe the situation. There are two units of clones circled around a huge bonfire, while they feast on Nate's livestock. There is at least a unit inside of Nate's house also, but there is no sign of John. Jake figures that he has to be in the house. He knows that if he can kill John, it will be all over. The clones around the fire will be easy pickings. They do not even have their rifles with them. Jake devises a plan that spreads his men out almost the entire way around the clones while he sneaks around to the front of the house. He gives his men a time to open fire on the clones while he lay in wait for John to be drawled outside by the commotion.

Everybody is in position and waiting for that first shot. Jake is behind a tree scanning everything for John's silhouette. He notices a figure appearing out of the dark and into the light of the fire. It's Nate, running full bore towards the circle of clones. He has his rifle in one hand and his pistol in the other. When he gets within twenty feet, he fires both weapons into the backs of two clones. The first two clones fall forward, and Nate jumps right over them as he fires two more bullets into another two clone's sides. Nate stands right in the middle of the circle, flipping his rifle down so he can work the lever action with one hand and pistol blazing in the other hand, like a madman. The clones are falling backwards trying to get away from Nate. They scramble to get to their assault rifles that are leaning against the house. Nate shoots eight clones dead before he runs out of bullets. A clone charges him only to meet the butt of Nate's rifle square in the face. The clone staggers backwards and trips over one of the logs that the clones were sitting on. The clone falls flat on its back with a thud. Nate is wildly swinging his rifle like a baseball bat at the rest of the clones, until two clones grab him from behind.

Ω

Jake cannot believe what he is seeing. His heart is pounding between his ears as he wonders what to do. He glances back at the house and sees a glimpse of John heading for the door to see his new prisoner. Jake locks his crosshairs on the doorway, ready to take John out. He glances back to Nate. The clone that Nate smashed in the face is very pissed off, and is storming up to Nate with a machete in its hand. Jake wants to give some kind of signal to his men to open fire, but does not want to give up his location and jeopardize his chance to get John. The clone stands right in front of Nate's face and slowly raises the machete high above its head, ready to sink it through Nate's skull. Jake is locked on to the doorway like a snapping turtle. He is going to take his shot at John no matter what. Jake tries to steady his rifle, but he feels like he has thousands of red-hot needles piercing through his skin from the inside out. Jake has a split second decision to make. He swings his rifle over and puts a bullet through the clone's head just as it's starting to strike Nate. Jake quickly swings the rifle back to the doorway only to see John diving back into the house.

The rest of Jake's men open fire on the clones. The two clones that are holding Nate throw him to the ground and run for their guns, to join their comrades in blindly firing into the woods. Nate sees his ATV with the shotgun still in the rack, and he races to get it. Jake figures that if he wasted his chance to get John, he is not going to let Nate get killed now. Jake charges back around the house to get Nate. Nate already had his shotgun and is firing from the hip by the time Jake gets to him. Nate is a man possessed by anger and hatred and is walking right into the crossfire of a heated battle as he blasts buckshot into any clone that he sees. The shotgun is quickly emptied and it's a good thing because Nate would have shot Jake when he grabs Nate from behind.

Jake is pulling Nate towards the woods, but Nate resists. Jake yells to Nate that they have to fall back to the ambush point. Nate screams, "Leave me alone, my family is dead and I'm gonna kill as many as those sons-a-bitches as I can." Nate storms back towards the house with his empty shotgun cocked back over his shoulder like it's a club. Jake can see it in his eyes that he is on a suicide mission and will not listen to reason. He clubs Nate on the back of his head, which knocks him out cold. Jake gathers him up and heads for the ambush point as he tries to wave his men to retreat. Once in the cover of the woods, Jake starts to second-guess his decision to save Nate instead of killing John. Jake is getting a sick feeling in his gut when he thinks about how many more people will die by John's hand because of one decision to save one man. Jake fears making wrong decisions more than he fears any clone. His latest decision fuels his fear even more.

Ω

Clones are slaughtered at two other locations during the night. One group of Jake's men even confiscate a tank, and they are bouncing it off of the guardrails going up the road as they try to figure out how to operate it. It takes all night for everybody to get back to the ambush point. John and the rest of the clones never set foot back outside of the house until morning. John pulls all of his units back to one location in the last town that he stormed through. It's wide-open landscape where nobody can sneak up on them. John needs some time to regroup and rethink his operation.

Ω

When Jake sees that John has retreated to town, he pulls his men back to the hotel, tank and all. John does not have enough soldiers to split up again, and Jake wonders if he is waiting for reinforcements. Some of Jake's men want to attack John in town, but Jake knows better than to get caught in the open with no cover. Moral is up and down from men worrying

154

that their victory was only against a scouting party, and the real army is on the way. Jake tries to raise the men's spirits with a speech. He tells them not to be scared of John and his soldiers. Jake tries the preacher's technique. He raises his fist in the air and forcefully says, "We all seen that they are not invincible and they were the ones who were scared last night. They are not God's army. If God wanted us dead, we would be dead." Jake hides the fact that he is not a man of faith. He is learning to use religion as a tool to infiltrate the minds of his men.

As the men think about what Jake has said, they start to become more confident. More men come rolling up the other side of the mountain later that afternoon, ready to join the fight. Everybody is happy to see more help arrive. Jake is very happy to see the new recruits, but he questions their ability to fight as a team, which will endanger the lives of everybody else. These people are from deep in the mountains. Jake can tell just by looking at them that they have just a little crazy in them. At any rate, the men bring more vehicles and supplies with them, which is a welcome sight.

Ω

Nate is basically held prisoner under suicide watch all day. Later that night as the men feast and get to know one another a little better, Jake tries to talk to Nate. He asks Nate what happened to his family, but Nate refuses to talk about it. Jake does not push the issue. He does try to convince Nate to take as much revenge as possible by fighting smart. Jake tells him not to be in such a hurry to die, it will happen on its own soon enough. Jake dismisses the man that is watching over Nate, and they both walk out of the room. Before Jake leaves the doorway he turns and says to Nate, "I don't know what you believe but I'm sure that your family is in heaven and most people say that if you commit suicide, you go to Hell. Just because you don't pull the trigger yourself, doesn't mean that you didn't commit suicide." Jake could never find the faith to believe in what just came out of his mouth, and he has his doubts that Nate is a believer, but it was worth a try.

In the morning Jake is glad to see Nate among the other men, and everybody seems to be in good spirits. Then the sound of a helicopter ripples through the air. Everybody scrambles to hide everything, but there are just too many vehicles, not to mention a tank. Jake runs to the lookout and hunkers down behind the rock wall to see what John is up to. John is flying low, bee-lining right for the hotel. Jake orders his men to scatter into the trees for cover, knowing full well that John will fire everything that he has into the whole place. John slowly hovers right over top of the trees and up along the mountain like he is trying to sneak up on the men. Jake has his rifle up and ready to put the crosshairs on John as soon as he pops up over the tree line.

Ω

John rises above the trees, and he is almost level with Jake. He never sees Jake because he is too busy looking at his stolen tank. Jake is starting to squeeze the trigger when he notices that there is somebody else in the helicopter with John. It's the preacher from the town below. He has ratted out Jake and his men. Jake is so angry that he must be subconsciously pulling his rifle over towards the preacher. He fires, and the bullet slices right between them. There is a little luck with Jake's shot though. The bullet hits something crucial in the helicopter. Jake can see sparks flying and smoke rolling as John fights to stabilize the helicopter. John flies back towards town and has to set down in a field halfway there.

Ω

The men all come running out of the woods cheering at their latest victory. Jake hates to burst their bubble, but he knows that there will be jet fighters screaming through the sky to blow the top of the mountain off. The men have to load everything that they have into their pickups and find someplace to hide. They disperse in both directions out the top of the mountain and set up in small discrete camps. The hotel is cleared out just in time. In a blink of an eye, two planes turn the militia headquarters into a giant fireball.

Ω

When the explosions are over and the planes long gone, Jake runs to the lookout to see what John is doing. Here he comes, in attack formation ready to charge up the mountain. Jake sees two units splitting off in both directions. He figures that they are going to cross the mountain on both sides and try to cut the men off and attack from behind. Jake orders his men to the three ambush sites. The main force barrels down the mountain ready to stop John from crossing the mountain at all costs. Men are also full throttle down over the other side of the mountain to cut off the flanking soldiers, but Jake has his doubts about whether or not they will make it in time. Jake sends a half a dozen men out the top of the mountain on foot in both directions across the rough terrain in a foot race to beat the flanking units. Their mission is to distract and slow the flanking units so that the rest of the men can engage the clones as low on the mountain as possible.

Jake joins the men below him at the ambush point to try and get a crack at John again. The men are just about to cut the trees across the road when one of them has an idea. They no longer have the element of surprise, so why not try to drop the trees on the clones instead of in front of them. The man explains to Jake what he has in mind. Jake commits to the plan. The men search for ropes, chains, and cables or anything that can support the weight of a tree. The men are prepared and surprisingly they have everything that they need in their pickups. They pick out three huge oak trees and tie them off to the butts of other trees with rope at the bottom so that it can be silently cut. The trees are then notched and almost cut through on the backside. When the ropes are cut, the trees will come crashing down. The trap is set and some of the men take the vehicles and equipment back up the road and out of sight.

As the men lay in wait for John, a chill comes across the air and it starts to drizzle rain. All in all, Jake is not really looking forwards to doing battle with John and the clones, but he is anxious to get it started. The longer the men lay still in the inclement weather, the more cold, sluggish, and unmotivated them become. Finally Jake can hear the rumble of John and his battalion coming up the road. John is unnerved at everything that seems to be unraveling around him again and quite pissed about his helicopter. He means business now and gives the order to shoot or blow up anything that moves. John plans to push through to Eden no matter what in order to regroup and reassess the situation. John also needs to find out what is going on in Eden and organize the assessment of all the children that he has been hauling into Eden. John envisions Eden being in turmoil due to thousands of kids that need taken care of.

Ω

John comes into sight of Jake and his men, and they forget how cold and wet they are. Their hearts are pounding, and the adrenaline warms their bodies. Jake is hidden back from the three trees and ready to give the order to cut them loose. He will attempt to line them up in order to disable as many vehicles and clones as possible. John has three tanks in a V formation in front, a long truck carrying clones next, and two armored, rubber tired vehicles in the rear. Jake has no idea where John is, or if he is even there. He figures that John is in one of the vehicles in the rear. But he is afraid to let the tanks get between the trees and his men's vehicles and supplies that are up around the turn.

John is moving at top speed and Jake no longer has time to think. He gives the order to cut the ropes. The ropes are cut and there is so much strain that they pop like gunshots, which causes Jake's men to open fire on the convoy. Jake tries to stop his men from firing. It's too late. John's bullet riddled convoy smashes on the brakes. Jake watches the trees that seem to be falling in slow motion. John's vehicles are still moving when the trees hit, but they have slowed enough that the trees are a little ahead of their targets. Jake is upset at his men and disappointed that the trees did not exactly hit their marks. His mind is busy racing back and forth trying to anticipate what is going to happen next.

Jake can't see what for damage has been done due to the treetops and smoke. It is clear by the sound of the trees hitting that they have done some damage to something. Everything in John's armada has hit reverse and is backing out of the treetops except the first tank and the one closest to Jake. The first tank has taken a direct hit from the tree trunk to the base of the barrel, ripping the turret loose from the rest of the tank. Jake focuses his eyes on the second tank and sees that its barrel is aimed right at him. As Jake realizes that the tank has him dead to rights, it fires. Jake dives backwards, spinning to his stomach. There is a very loud explosion, and Jake feels the blast on his backside. He lay face down for a few seconds until he realizes that he is still alive, and not even mangled. The second tree had barely hit the barrel of the tank but was enough to bend the barrel. The shell never left the tank. The tank blew apart like a soda can with a firecracker exploding inside it.

Jake is an optimist and pretty happy about taking out two of the three tanks. The personnel carrier truck is also out of commission from being waylaid with bullets. Everything else is in perfect working order and throwing some serious firepower into the tree lines where the men are taking cover. The clone foot soldiers have pretty good cover behind the armored vehicles, and there is not much to shoot at. The rain is turning into snow. The mountain seemed to grab the passing clouds and hold them overhead as a spine tingling chill falls across the air. Jake calls for his men to retreat. The retreat plan is for both sides of the road to make large circles through the woods and rendezvous back on the road at the next ambush site. Jake is watching his men across the road scurry up over the bank, except for Nate. He is still kneeling behind a tree and pumping lead into John's convoy. Just as Jake gives up on him and is about to retreat, Nate jumps up, nods his head at Jake, and takes off up through the brush.

By now it's snowing large, heavy, wet flakes so hard that the men can only see thirty feet in front of them. It is like a thick fog. The men group together and slow to a walk. There is already an inch or two of snow on the ground, and everything is dead silent. All of the men are come over with an eerie feeling. The guy in the rear can't help looking behind him every ten seconds. He catches a glimpse of something moving through the trees below. He yells out, and the men quickly take cover behind the trees with their rifles to their shoulders. The heavy snow, large trees, and lack of sunshine make it almost impossible for the men to see any sign of a threat. After a few minutes, the men dismiss the threat as a deer and they start moving again.

The more the guy runs the image that he saw through his mind, the more convinced he becomes that it was no deer. It's snowing harder than ever now, and the men are trudging up through the snow in single file. The last guy is still constantly looking behind himself and getting more nervous with every step. He notices that the men in front of him are making a slight turn around a huge pine tree. He can't see them for a while until they appear on the other side. He reaches the mammoth tree and smoothly rolls around against it. He slowly peeks out around to see if anything is following them. He watches nothing but a few dark silhouettes of trees in the vast whiteout for a minute or so. He decides that he does not want to fall too far behind the other men. He rolls around on the tree to his back, to push off the tree and start trudging up through the snow again. His eyes lock on a clone standing three feet in front of him. Before he even has a chance to scream, the clone takes a large double-bladed axe and chops through his neck. His body slides down the tree to the ground in pile of lifeless flesh. His head still sits on top of the embedded ax until the clone removes its' weapon from the tree.

Ω

John had seen the men retreating up over the side of the mountain and sent a team of clones to run them down and kill them. John also knows that there are men on the other side of the road but can't see them down over the bank. By the time the clones secure that side of the road, Jake and his men have already started circling around. The clones can't track them in the quickly falling snow. None of the other men have any idea that the clones are tracking them down or that they have just lost a man. A clone is silently running up behind the last man. As quick as a lightning, the clone grabs the man's head and twists, snapping his neck like a twig. The rest of the men have their hoods up and toboggans on and never hear a thing.

Finally the next man looks back and sees that the two men that were behind him are missing. He halts the rest of the men. They all just stand there dumbfounded for a minute, until they realize that they are under attack. They quickly take cover behind the trees with their rifles pointed down the mountain. The men stare into the snowy void in dead silence for several minutes. The man on the outside position fires off a shot. The other men look over and see him lying face down with a very large knife sticking out of his back. All of the men look at each other in fear and then look towards the outside man on the other side. He is also face down in the snow. There are only three men left. Panic sets in as they start to blindly fire their rifles off into the falling snow in every direction. The three eventually sit down in the open with their backs towards each other so they can see an attack coming from any direction. The clones leave the men sit there, profusely shaking from cold and fear, for about ten minutes before they shoot the terrified men.

Ω

Nate has lost track of the other men in the storm and makes a much wider circle than the others, which saves his life. He heard the gunshots though and cautiously heads towards them to investigate. When Nate gets there the clones are long gone, but the three men are still sitting up, leaning against one another, with their rifles to their shoulders. The men have the most pitiful look on their faces, and Nate can't stand to look at them. He searches for survivors until he finds all of the men's bodies. The snow stops, but it is starting to get dark. Nate hurries off to the rendezvous point.

$$\Omega$$

Jake and the rest of the men have been nervously waiting for two hours to see the men appear out of the woods. Eventually Nate shows up and tells everybody what he has found. All of the men were becoming pretty confident and fearless of the clones, but Nate's story puts the fear right back into them. Jake's flanking forces do pretty well with their missions. Both sides have immobilized the armored vehicles with trees in front, behind, and on top of them. Men on both flanks selflessly gave their lives to do so. The flanking men did not have the ropes or the idea of precutting the trees. Once the initial trees were cut to stop the clones, the men stood in gunfire while they cut the trees meant to disable and trap the convoy. When one man fell with a saw in his hands, another quickly took his place. The men got the job done, and the clones are trapped inside of their armored vehicles. It's a deadly standoff that will last throughout the night.

Throughout the night, Jake has trouble dealing with his guilt of so many men dying while following his orders. Everybody is down-hearted, but it's the men who try to cheer Jake up this time. It's a little hard to be optimistic when you have to keep one eye peeled open for John and his clones coming up the road to slaughter you. Nate is sitting all by himself and not saying a word, as usual, but he is watching Jake. Nate is not a man of many words, but he approaches Jake and tells him that none of the men gave their lives for him. They fought to protect their homes and families. There is an awkward moment of silence until Nate says, "If we don't follow through and stop that crazy nut down there, they died for nothing." Nate starts to walk away, then stops and says to Jake, "I should have listened to you." Nate's comment makes Jake realize that the whole country is in turmoil. There are millions of people who have lost much more and are feeling a whole lot worse than he is. The only thing to do is stop John. Jake becomes more determined than ever.

Ω

John decides to wait until morning to proceed up the mountain. He knows that his flanking units are lost, and he still can't make contact with Eden. Some fresh clones are starting to show up here and there across the country but nowhere near to being on schedule. There has to be a major problem at Eden. Without John's helicopter, there is only one way for him to get there. Jake and his men stopping John in his tracks is just enough to start pushing him over the edge. John calls off his tactical sweeping of the country and orders his quadrant commanders to pull all the units together in one location. Once the clones are all together, they are to be split in half. One half will be sent to re-man the military bases in the quadrant, and the other half are to push through to Eden.

In the morning John will push up and over the mountain at all costs.

Early in the morning, John's only reinforcements arrive in four Hummers. John knows that he is fighting an uphill battle, so he sends his reinforcements north to circle around behind Jake to attack from the rear. There is a four-lane highway that travels underneath the mountain through tunnels about twenty miles to the north. John orders his reinforcements to approach the tunnels on foot, scout them out, and secure them. Once the tunnels are secure, the clones can sneak through the tunnels with their vehicles and race south to engage Jake from the other side. John realizes that the tunnels would be an excellent location for an ambush, but he figures that nobody will think he is foolish enough to travel through them. He also hopes that he has all of the men drawled into one location to meet him head on. Nobody will even realize that the smaller, faster vehicles are flanking around the mountain. John does not know that Jake always has someone watching from the lookout. Jake sends a small team to track the flanking clones and to engage if necessary.

Ω

Jake and his men are set up to meet John head-on about a mile up the road. They have their confiscated tank hidden along the road ready to fire into the other tank. Jake's tank only has two shells, and they will both have to count. Their only chance is to take out John's tank first. Jake's tank men are under tremendous pressure, and they are starting to wish that they had never even taken the thing. Their stress presents them with an idea. The road is a long sweeping turn cut into the side of a steep slope. There is a high cliff right along side of the road on the inside of the turn. If they move the tank across and on down the road a little piece, they will be shooting into the side of the cliff. Even if they miss John's tank, the shell will hit the cliff and hopefully start a landslide. The second shell can be fired into the cliff regardless and possibly take out the rest of John's fleet. Jake loves the idea and tells the men to get on it.

The men quickly move the tank and are backing it up into position. Some of the other men drag rocks, brush, and anything else they can get a hold of onto the road to push John over to the lane beside the cliff. The tank operators are carefully lining up the tank and backing it behind some brush to hide. All of a sudden the tank driver is looking straight in the sky and sliding backwards down over a steep bank. The tank stops abruptly when it slides into a deep washed out gully. The tank can't go backwards because of the gully, and it can't climb the steep, loose, slate bank in front of it. It is hopelessly stuck. Jake cannot believe what has just happened. He was so proud of the men for the great idea. Now, he wants to strangle them for screwing it up.

The sun is already high in the sky and shining brightly. It's much warmer and most of the snow is already gone. Jake knows that John will be coming around the turn full bore at any time and without the tank, they will not have a chance. Jake and his men will have to retreat on up the mountain to where the road narrows and cut some more trees across the road. Jake orders the men to take both of the shells out of the tank and everybody else needs to scramble up the mountain. Jake asks for a volunteer to stay and try to draw attention to the disabled tank in order to buy them some time. A fellow that come out of the mountains, named Jim, volunteers to stay along with a handful of other men, including the ones who lost the tank. They are desperate to make up for their moment of stupidity. Jake tells them to just get John and the clones to notice the tank, and that's all. Then get up the mountain as fast as they can.

Meanwhile, both flanks are still in their standoff. The men decide to burn the clones out of their armored vehicles. The men find whatever they can to hold gasoline to throw on the vehicles, along with torches. The armor that protects the clones will not burn. The paint starts to peel off from the heat, and the men know that it has to be like an oven inside. It takes a while, but eventually the clones make a run for it. The hatches fly open, and the big machine guns on the assault vehicles are laying down cover fire. The clones are jumping out so fast and going in every direction that it is hard for the men to pick them off. The smoke from their fires is hindering the men's vision. The clones take heavy losses, but there are still a few from each flank that gets away and head for John.

Jim and the others pretty much ignore Jake's orders and have made plans of their own. The man who drove the tank down over the bank, stretches out some logging chains on the road and down over the bank. He then plans to wait there until the clones see him and then run down over the bank, leading the clones to the tank. He only removes one shell and plans to shoot the other one at whatever shows up at the top of the bank. While Jim is strapping two emp-ty water barrels onto the roof of his pickup, he ex-plains to the other men that he will create a diversion while they open fire on John's convoy and then re-treat up the mountain in the remaining truck.

Jim can hear John coming just out of sight around the turn. There is a third truck lane in the road, but Jim figures that John will be single-file in the center lane with the clones on foot between the vehicles. Jim has an old four-wheel drive, rusted out Chevy with a snowplow on it. He jumps in, pops in his favorite cassette tape, finds his favorite song and cranks up the volume. He buckles his seat belt, throws his arm up on the windowsill and smashes the throttle to the floor. The other men just look at each other thinking that will be the last time they will ever see Jim. They slowly follow him in the other truck, ready to make a fast U-turn and flee up the mountain.

Jim is flying down the road in the inside lane. When John's tank comes into sight, Jim sees that its barrel is aimed at the top of the bank, suspecting another ambush. John's formation is exactly as Jim had thought. The tank starts swinging its barrel to-wards him. Jim starts veering over to the outside lane while he concentrates intensely on the barrel. Jim's old truck is going as fast as it can. Jim stares right down the barrel of the tank. As soon as the barrel stops, Jim cuts the steering wheel back towards the inside lane. The tank fires but misses Jim. The shell screams by so close that it knocks the mirror off the door and singes the hair on Jim's arm. He is bearing down hard on the tank, and it becomes clear that the tank will not get another shot off. With the barrels on the truck's roof, the clones think that Jim is a kamikaze bomber. They scatter to get away from the tank. Right before Jim hits the tank, he whips the truck over into the other lane. He starts mowing down clones with his snowplow, not once leaving off the throttle. He drives right around the whole convoy and keeps on going down the road. The tank swings its barrel around after him but can't shoot because of the vehicles behind it. Jim does take a lot of rifle fire from everything else as he drives away.

The men in the other pickup cannot believe their eyes and almost miss their opportunity to take out some clones. They fire until the tank starts to swing back around towards them, and they take off back up over the mountain. The truck stops and backs up to the log chains. They sit there until the lead tank sees them and then take off again. The two guys who lost the tank stay and act like they are pulling the chain up over the bank. They come under fire and dive down over the bank. John's convoy reaches the chain, and they stop. Two clones peek down over the bank, and when they see the tank they dive backwards looking for cover.

John figures that it's another ambush, so he sends clones to circle around behind the tank to thwart the attack. John waits for the sound of gunshots or the clones' return. The clones find the tank empty and try to climb the bank. The slate keeps kicking out underneath the tracks, digging it in deeper and deeper. The clones run up the bank to tell John the news and to get the winch line from the other tank to pull it out. John is ecstatic that he finally catches a break and is getting his tank back. He cracks the whip on the clones and wants his tank out immediately. Then they will charge up the mountain with nothing to worry about but falling trees.

All of the clones are up at the top of the bank and backing their tank up to the edge. The two men are hiding in the gully about twenty feet above the tank. One of them sneaks down and into the tank while the other covers him. When the tank on the road backs up to the edge of the bank, the man inside of the disabled tank can sight right up underneath its belly. Just as a clone starts to walk behind the tank to grab the winch line, the guy in the disabled tank fires its one and only round. It's a direct hit to the undercarriage, which blows the tracks clean off both sides taking out another half-dozen clones. The two men quickly sneak up the gully and into the woods and are never seen by John or his clones.

Ω

John comes unglued and starts screaming and kicking in the middle of the road. His tantrum lasts until he is exhausted. He sits in the middle of the road thinking about how his quest is falling to pieces. He is all set to travel back down the mountainside and try a different road up over, until his anger and pride gets in the way of logical thinking. John is torn between getting to Eden and crushing the resistance. Even if he does get to Eden, he still has people opposing him and does not have total control. That is a major problem for John. He comes up with a plan to end the resistance once and for all.

John turns what is left of his battalion around and heads for the town down in the valley. John orders the clones to take twenty prisoners. With the help of the preacher, seven of the prisoners have intimate knowledge of or are helping the resistance. John takes his new prisoners back to the foot of the mountain and locks them inside a fence that is around an electric substation. He sends one prisoner up the mountain to find Jake and tell him that starting first thing in the morning one prisoner will die every morning until they all surrender.

The flanking clones are slowly and cautiously securing the tunnels. The men know that they cannot let the clones pass through to the other side of the mountain. A few of the men commandeer a fuel truck from a local oil company. They plan to try and blow the end of the tunnels shut so the clones can't get through. The men have the fuel truck just out of sight from the end of the tunnel and are trying to figure out how to do the job without someone dying in a suicide mission. The men wish that they could trap the clones inside of the tunnel, but it will be hard enough just to block one end. Finally the clones have the tunnels secure. The men will have to make their move, ready or not. Just as one man makes the decision to sacrifice himself and drive the tanker into the end of the tunnels, the clones all leave together and start walking back to get their vehicles.

The men watch in disbelief as the clones disappear out of sight. They figure that the clones are not going to pass through after all. The men are not going to take any chances and quickly park the truck inside the tunnel. They can detonate the truck by shooting into the tank, and nobody will have to die. One man is still following the clones and sees that they are heading for the tunnel. He radios the men that they are on their way. The men think of a better plan and quickly open the drain valve on the tank. They drive through the tunnel spewing hundreds of gallons of fuel all over the road.

The clones blindly race their hummers into the tunnel, anxious to join the fight with John. When the clones are about half way through the tunnel, the men light the fuel in front of them. Flames shoot up to the ceiling inside of the tunnel. The clones stand on the brakes and slide to a stop. As soon as the clones realize that the flames are racing towards them, they hit reverse and smash the throttle to the floor. All four of the hummers are going as fast as they can backwards. The clones watch the wall of fire gaining on them. The last vehicle, which is actually now the front vehicle, starts to swerve out of control. It spins sideways and the next vehicle slams into it, wedging them both against the walls of the tunnel. The other two vehicles, who have a front row seat to the skin melting wall of fire that is quickly bearing down on them, push into the wedged vehicles to break through and escape. The road is wet from the fuel and hindering traction. The pile up is just slowly sliding through the tunnel. Smoke is rolling off the spinning tires. Clones are screaming in fear and in pain from being pinned between crashed vehicles. The clones are desperately digging and clawing to get out of their crumpled vehicles, but their comrades keep ramming into them. The fire relentlessly tracks them down. Two clones from the front vehicle jump out, leap over the wreckage, and try to out run the fire on foot. As they run they can feel the heat singeing the hair off of their bodies. They hear their comrades screaming at the top of their lungs, followed by multiple explosions as the fire consumes the wreckage.

After the fire dies down, the men walk through the tunnel. The men find all four vehicles and actually feel a little sorry for the clones that are still trapped in their hummers, burnt to a crisp.

Ω

Jake and his men are on the mountainside celebrating their latest victories and the fact that they do not have to deal with any more tanks. The fellow who lost the tank has gone from jeopardizing the whole militia to being the biggest hero so far, all in one day. Jim even eventually shows up without a scratch on him, although he does need a new truck. The celebration is cut short when the prisoner comes and tells the men what John is doing. Jake immediately takes Nate and a couple other local boys and heads for the substation. Jake fears a trap, so he orders the rest of the men to stay put until they hear from him and to be ready in case John shows up.

It is morning until Jake and the others make it to the substation. John has all nineteen prisoners lined up along the fence and facing nineteen clones on the other side of the fence. John walks behind the clones and chooses a prisoner to execute by poking the clone opposite of the prisoner in the back. John knows the seven that the preacher picked and will save them for last. They are his bargaining chips. He chooses the insignificant ones to prove that he means business. John drags the execution out for as long as he can, mainly to torture the terrified prisoners. The prisoner's anticipation of whether or not they will be the one executed is worse than being shot. John preaches for about half an hour. He then walks to the end of the firing squad, steps back, and he stands there in silence for at least another five minutes. Each minute seems like an hour, and most of the prisoners tremble in fear more uncontrollably with each passing minute. Finally, John gives the order to fire. The chosen clone pulls up and shoots the prisoner opposite from it.

Ω

Two of the men with Jake are local brothers. When the prisoners turn around to walk away from the dead body, the brothers notice that their father is a prisoner. Jake has to hold the youngest brother down to keep him from charging in to rescue his dad. The young man pleads with Jake to do something to help his father. Jake knows that they cannot surrender, but he also knows that they cannot let the innocent people be tortured and ruthlessly executed. The men come up with a simple plan to free the prisoners. Two of them will cause a diversion while the other two will cut the fence and quietly free the prisoners.

Once it's dark, Jake and Nate move around to the other side of the substation to start the diversion. The two brothers prepare to cut the fence with a pair of bolt cutters that they have stolen out of a nearby shed. There is a clone stationed at every corner of the fence on guard. The younger brother is fretting about the guards, but the older brother assures him that the guards will leave their posts to go after Jake and Nate. When the commotion finally starts, there is a lot of gunfire being exchanged that lights up the night sky. John has expected exactly what is happening, and the guards do not move a muscle. In an act of desperation, the brothers shoot the two guards. They are hoping that their gunshots were muffled by the roar of the machine guns and will go unnoticed. They do not get halfway to the fence until they come under heavy fire themselves. Miraculously neither one of them is hit, but a bullet takes the bolt cutters right out of the younger one's hands. They are forced to retreat into the woods for cover.

Jake, Nate, and the brothers rendezvous the next morning just in time to watch John's line up. This time, after the same performance, John yells fire, and two clones pull up and shoot two prisoners. John then yells out, "Every time that you try something like last night, two will die the next morning." Jake has his crosshairs on John the whole time, but cannot get a clear shot. John makes sure that he has a clone barrier around himself at all times. The older brother notices a couple of things that will work to their advantage during a rescue. The four have a lengthy discussion and come up with another plan. The older brother is an excellent marksman with a very high-powered rifle. He and Jake spread out and watch the substation for John to poke his head out at some point during the day. The other two go back up the mountain to get the required men and equipment for their plan. The preacher from town shows up and spends the whole day giving sermons to the prisoners. He really works on the seven to confess their sins and give up information on the resistance. He turns the rest of the prisoners against the seven in order to save their lives.

All night the men move into their positions. John is expecting another night attack, so he and his clones are on high alert. The men have to be a little

more careful getting into position without being de-
tected. Just before dawn everybody is ready and
waiting. At first light, John calls for his lineup. He is
making his usual dramatic scene. The clone firing
squad is in a perfect line, and Jake and the older
brother are lined up perfectly with the clones on both
ends. John always walks away from the clones,
turns, and then yells fire. When John turns this time,
Jake and the brother fire into the firing squad. They
both are aiming for the clone's necks, and the older
brothers high-powered rifle bullet blazes through four
clone necks and lodges in the fifth one. Jake's bullet
only takes out two clones on the other end, and the
rest of Jake's snipers open up on the clones. The
prisoners hit the dirt as two pickups fly up over the
bank and around to the back of the substation. The
pickups have men in the back firing on the clones,
including the younger brother who has an extra rifle
which he lobes over the fence to his father. One of
the trucks backs through the fence laying it flat to the
ground. They back through the fence keeping the
large transformers inside of the substation between
them and John's armored vehicles, which provides
them with cover from the mounted machine guns.

The clones are under fire from all directions,
even inside the fence. John has scurried for cover
with the first shot, and it does not take the clones
long to retreat to the armored vehicles right behind
him. The prisoners are diving behind the large transformers, then in single file loading into the two pickups. John's heavy machine guns blaze into the transformers but are not reaching the pickups. The pickups can't escape straight away for the woods. If they
go out the way that they come in, they will be cut to

shreds. The large transformers are starting to hiss and whistle while they heave in and out. The escaping men are starting to think that the transformers that have been protecting them are becoming as much of a threat as the clones. They are definitely between a rock and a hard place. Just as the prisoners and their rescuers are about to make a run for it on foot, the older brother notices something else. John has his assault vehicles parked right under the transmission line that feeds the substation. The older brother takes aim at the thick wire and within three shots he severs it. The wire falls out of the sky and lands on one of John's armored vehicles, blowing the rubber tires clean off in a ground-shaking explosion. As giant fireballs roll up into the sky the pickups seize the opportunity and escape. In a matter of seconds everybody is gone, and everything is quiet.

Ω

John is furious again, but also quite shaken at how close he had just come to losing his life again. Within days, his war machine has been reduced to one assault vehicle and thirteen soldiers. John is out of options and wants to run to the safety of Eden. The tables have turned now, and John is afraid of becoming the hunted instead of the hunter. John is blundering around the smoking substation as he tries to comprehend his situation. He notices the preacher from town standing there with three of the prisoners. The prisoners figure that it will be safer to stand beside John than against him. They all know that Jake or his men will not purposely kill them either way.

John just stands there and blankly stares at the four of them. The preacher starts into one of his mini sermons, until he realizes that it is perturbing John. Truth is, the preacher is really stepping on John's toes. John feels that if there is any preaching to be done, he will be the one doing it. The preacher then nervously says to John, "These three have decided to join us." John questions the preacher by saying, "join....us?" John slowly bends over and pulls an assault rifle out of the hands of a dead clone. The four men's eyes become as big as saucers when they realize that they are in big trouble. The three prisoners take off running for their lives. John mows them down through their backs. The preacher starts stuttering and stammering around with his hands up as if he is trying to stop John. John puts one bullet into the preacher's guts, and he falls to the ground in pain. John then leans over and tells him that he will have some time to think about where he has went wrong and to make peace with God before he dies.

John storms to the assault vehicle and calls in a massive air strike. His gives orders to decimate everything within five hundred feet on both sides of the road, the whole way up the mountain. John will charge through right behind the explosions. It does not take long until the mountain is shaking like an earthquake. Jake and his men can see the rolling fireballs getting closer and closer to them. The men know that it is a battle that they do not stand a chance at, and they will have to run for their lives. Jake tries to tell the men to abandon their trucks and flee into the woods on foot. Some listen to him, but most pile onto a truck and race for position up over the mountain.

The planes quickly see the convoy of pickups floor boarding up over the mountain. John orders them to be destroyed, as he starts up the mountain. One by one the pickups are blown into nothing right up the line from the back. The men can see their comrades getting picked off behind them, which starts a frenzied panic. When one truck gets passed by a faster truck, two of the men in the back start to throw the other men off the back, just to lose weight and gain some speed. The truck behind swerves to attempt to miss the men rolling on the road but still run over one man, never lifting off of the throttle. As the two that are dumping weight look out over top of the cab, they are happy to see that they are gaining on the rest of the pack. They turn back around just in time to see a rocket flying right into their laps.

Realizing that they should have listened to Jake, some of the men start jumping off the sides just to get away from the trucks. Most do not survive smashing into the road at eighty miles an hour. The rest are run over by the trucks behind them. By the time the lead truck reaches the top of the mountain, they are all lost but one. The men in the last pickup keep looking up ahead and then behind in shear desperation, praying that they will make it to the crest of the mountain before another plane catches them. They are finally cresting the top. They look behind and see a plane bearing down on them, but it's too far away. The planes rockets will never reach them in time before they barrel down over the other side of the mountain. As they scream out in pure joy, the men turn around to watch in front of them as they head down the slope. They catch sight of a plane that has already made its run and flying back over them. A split second later they notice a small glimmering object leaving a vapor trail right into their radiator. Not one man escapes.

Ω

Jake and the rest of the men on foot have come to what has to be at least a ten-acre rock field on the side of the mountain. Jake is sure that the outcropping was not there before. They are hesitant to cross in the open, but they are desperate to get away from the noise of death and destruction behind them. At that point they want to get as far away from the road as possible, as quick as possible. It will take too long to go around the rock field. Emotions from all of their friends being killed are clouding their judgment, and they start across the rocks. A plane immediately spots the men and reports it to John, who orders a strike on the men. The planes wait for Jake and the men to get right in the middle of the wide-open rock field before they fly in for the attack. The men see the plane bearing down on them and instantly realize that they are all about to die. There is nothing that any of them can do about it. Some men try to run across the very large rubble rock, some ball up into the fetal position, and some just close their eyes and pray. Jake, Nate, and a few others just stand there and watch. Just as the plane is about to open fire on the men, it explodes in mid air and falls into the trees before the men in multiple flaming pieces.

The plane no sooner hits the ground when another plane screams through the air right over the men's heads. Then two more of John's planes explode over top of the road. The men see what appears to be dog fights out over the valley and back and forth across the mountain. It quickly becomes obvious that three fighter jets have just taken out John's whole fleet in a blink of an eye. The men are scared and confused as the three planes fly towards them in formation. The planes start to roll side to side as if they are waving at the men with their wings. The planes blow over the men's heads and disappear over the mountain.

Jake is smiling from ear to ear as he turns to his men and says, "Finally, the cavalry has arrived."

CHAPTER EIGHT
FALL FROM GLORY

John is sitting on the road, completely dumb-founded over what is happening. He manages to gather enough wits about him to get out of his assault vehicle and head into the woods for cover. John and the clones no sooner reach the tree line when one of the fighters swoop down and blow John's last piece of transportation and safety into a smoking pile of twisted metal. John does not want to believe it, but there is no other explanation. The military has to be attacking. With John's defenses in shambles, he does not stand a chance. John starts to feel the fear that he has been instilling into everyone else for the last six months. He tries to come to grips with the fact that he has lost control of everything and has just become the most wanted fugitive in history.

Ω

The military has been slowly infiltrating the country for months. The clones are too busy watching the seas for ships and the air for planes to see the troops walking right into the bases. The troops have taken back every military base in the country, one by one. The troops retook the bases with such stealth that

John has no idea the entire military is in the country. Most of the clones were dead before they even knew that they are being attacked. John has basically only been in contact with and using the one airfield for his bombing raids. The airfield was the only base that was any kind of a threat to the military, so they saved it for last to make sure that they had a good foothold inside the country. The military launched its strike against the airfield moments after John launched his strike against Jake and his men.

All throughout the country, John and his army are quickly finding out just who is in charge. The military is hunting down clones with great efficiency and with plenty of help from the citizens. John is trying to warn his quadrant commanders, but they are already finding out the hard way. John can hear the fear and panic in his commander's voices as they turn into screams and gunshots. John's army is on the run, and they do not have a clue of where they are running too. John is huddled against a tree, scared to death. He is thinking that the best thing for him to do is to try and get out of the country. Something keeps drawing him to Eden though. Eden is his creation, his home, and he has a strange sense of security there.

John gathers himself up and he and the clones head up the mountain on foot. John is running to Eden and figures that he will at least get over the scorched mountain unopposed. With any kind of luck, everyone will think that he is dead inside of the bombed assault vehicle. It's a long, slow walk up the mountain for John. Eventually he makes it. Just as John is walking across the top, Jake and his men come walking out of the woods right in front of John.

They all catch each other off guard. Both sides just stand there, not knowing what to do. After a second or two, Jake and the men run for the woods. John dives for the ditch along the road. The clones run nowhere and start shooting at the men. The men run down over the side of the mountain, staying in the trees and off of the road. John and the clones quickly chase after them. John can't keep up. The clones could easily run the men down, but every time that John starts to fall behind, he gets scared and holds the clones back.

John finally splits the clones up and sends half hot on the men's tails while the rest protect him as he hobbles along through the woods. John tries so hard to keep up but with every step he becomes more winded. He starts to feel intense pain in his hips. The fact that the war that he created has just left him behind like he is not even part of it, adds insult to injury. John finally has to stop and rest. John only rests for a couple of minutes until the pops of gunfire start to echo up across the mountain. John gets a shot of adrenaline, which pushes him up off the ground and down over the mountain again.

The men make it to the bottom of the mountain and take up a defensive position in a large abandoned stone farmhouse. The clones are bearing down on the men amazingly fast. They have no choice but to trap themselves in the old house just to have a fighting chance.

The men are on the second floor, shooting at the clones through the windows and pinning them behind the trees. The two sides are throwing a lot of lead at each other but not accomplishing anything. John finally shows up at the old house an hour later just as it's starting to get dark. It's a very long night with occasional barrages of gunfire. Every once in a while, a clone will try to sneak into the house, but the men are watching like a hawk and holding them back. The men stare intensely into the night trying to focus their eyes in the dark. They can hear the clones moving around the sides and to the back, completely surrounding the house. Jake and the others have been debating whether or not to sneak out the back of the house and slip off into the night, but that is not an option now. The men start to blindly fire at every noise that they hear in the surrounding woods.

Ω

John sits in the dark, curled up in a ball against a tree trying not to think about how tired, cold, and hungry he is. The more he thinks about what has happened over the past few days, the more paranoid he becomes. He feels like he should run for his life through the woods, but he is too scared to move. John is slipping into a state of shear desperation. He wishes that he never even tried to start his own church. He still is not feeling guilty for murdering millions of people, just worried about his own life. Finally, John notices that he can see better and better. Someone sees something that they can shoot at, and the sharp roar of battle is pounding in John's head again. The two sides waste ammunition for about ten minutes. It seems like an hour to John. Just as quick as it started, everybody goes right back into a dead silent standoff. John is shivering uncontrollably and cannot figure out why he is colder now than in the middle of the night. He has had enough. He does not have the time or the conviction to wait out a siege. John commands his soldiers to starve the men out or flat out kill them, just make sure that they all die. He picks out two clones to escort him, and they circle around the house and down through the woods heading for Eden.

Ω

Jake can see John and the two clones circling around the house. He is moving from one window to the next, trying to get a shot off at John. John keeps his distance though, and in Jake's frustration he exposes himself to a clone. The clone quickly shoots, and Jake flies backwards to the floor. Fearing the worst, the men furiously fire into the trees that are hiding the clone. The bullet only splits Jake's ear, and other than that, he is fine. He is a little shaken at how close he had come to losing his head because he was not using it. Jake tries to tape his ear back together while he thinks about how bad it sucks to have went toe to toe with John and his mutant soldiers and survive, only to die after the military has retaken the country. Everybody is cold, tired, and hungry. Jake knows that it will come down to who can last the longest, or who runs out of bullets first.

Ω

By noon the clones run out of ammunition. The men are dangerously low themselves. The clones spend the next hour sprinting from tree to tree, drawing the men's fire and depleting their ammunition. Eventually the men are running out, but Jake gets them to save one or two shells each. The clones are not looking forward to another hunger-filled night on the damp ground, so they charge the house, one by one, for a hand-to-hand fight. The men can't resist taking crack shots at the rushing clones and miss almost all of them. There are ten clones on the porch, ready to take on the men. The men have five rifles with one shell each and outnumber the clones almost two to one, but when the bullets are gone the men will not stand a chance against the clones.

As the men try to figure out a strategic plan to survive the clones, they attempt to stay optimistic. The conversation always goes back to the fact that they are only prolonging the inevitable. When the bullets run out, the men will only have a handful of pocketknives to do hand to hand combat with the clones. The clones all have machetes and axes and will never quit until they fulfill their orders, even if there is only one left. Then Jim jumps to his feet and says, "I have a wife and three kids and nobody is keeping me from going home. This damn war is over and I'm not getting killed now." Jim stands around the corner at the top of the stairs, with his rifle, prancing as adrenaline pumps through his body. The stairs go halfway up to a landing and turn one hundred and eighty degrees to go the rest of the way up to the second floor. The house is eerily quiet until the men hear the clones start to sneak up the stairs.

Another man gives Jim his rifle so that he will at least have two shots to charge the clones. Jake, Nate, and a few others line up behind Jim to make the charge. Jake tells the rest of the men that when the fighting starts, they are to bail out the windows and make a run for it. A step creaks at the top of the stairs. Jim launches his attack. Jim rounds the corner and fires into the first clone. As the first clone falls backwards, Jim fires the second rifle into the next clone. He throws the empty rifle at the third clone while he bends over to grab a weapon off of the second dead clone. The empty rifle bounces off the clone as it charges Jim with a machete raised to strike him down. Jake shoots right over Jim's head and into the third clone's chest, just in time. Jake tries to stay out of the way so the last two rifles can pass by him while he grabs weapons off of the dead clones. Jim wheels around the corner on the landing and thrusts a machete into another clone's stomach. The clone takes a swipe at Jim and slices his arm open as it falls to the stairs. The men stumble down the stairs trying to run over top of the dead clones. Nate rounds the corner to see Jim about to take on the next clone. Nate quickly shoots the clone. As it falls backwards, Jim dives headfirst right over the falling clone and sinks an axe into the skull of the next clone.

By now there is a pile of bodies entangled at the bottom of the stairs. The sound of bloodshed and battle fills the house. As Jim desperately tries to get to his feet, the last bullet rips through a clone that is about to butcher him. The men are stumbling down the stairs and gathering weapons while Jim dodges relentlessly swinging blades. One by one the men reach the bottom and team up against the clones. Their attacks quickly turn into defensive actions. Things are very congested between the stairs and the door with weapons slashing everywhere. The men groan and yell in exhaustion while they push their bodies to fight for their lives. A quiet young man, that nobody ever really got to know, launches off of the stairs and comes flying through the air with his empty rifle. He screams the most horrific war cry that anybody has ever heard and thrusts the barrel of his gun right through the eye of a clone. The young man lands on top of the bellowing clone and is immediately decapitated by another clone. Two other men fall before they kill two of the three clones at the bottom of the stairs. The last clone is now outside and holding the men from coming through the front door. Some of the men did bail out of the upstairs windows but instead of running, they gather up rocks and start pelting the last clone from behind. The clone turns to defend itself. Jim lunges and drives a machete into the clones back. Jim's adrenaline is pumping so hard that he runs around in circles three times in front of the house while slashing his blade through the air. The other men cautiously get him shut down, and he collapses to the ground.

Jim has seven slices and puncture wounds, but all of them are superficial. He is now only referred to as Lucky Jim. Jim and the other men's wounds are being treated while the rest gather the dead and are searching the bodies for supplies. The men notice that there is a clone body missing. Nobody really knows how many clones there were for sure, but just about all of the men think that there was another one. Nobody wants to stick around and search. They quickly follow John's trail down through the woods.

Ω

Jake and the men come to a farm and soon learn that John had been there looking for food. The farmer recognized him from TV and put him on the run with a shotgun. John wants to keep a low profile the whole way to Eden, so he kept his guard clones hidden and stole the family van. The men fill their bellies with food and water, and they decide to go after John. With being that close to John and as unprotected as he is, the men have a good chance to seal his fate. They do not want to take any chances by assuming that the military will capture him. The men stock up on as many supplies as the farm can spare, load up in a cattle truck, and head for Eden looking for John. Nobody really knows exactly where Eden is, but they figure that they can get close enough to find it.

The men soon find themselves in a small town where John had stopped to get gas. After filling up, he went inside the store, loaded up with food, and tried walking out without paying for anything. The clerk jumped the counter and stopped John at the door. There was a struggle. John managed to break away from the clerk and fled down the road in the van. Jake and the men receive plenty of help from the small town in the way of vehicles and weapons to run John down. Now the men can split up and make their own little sweep across the countryside searching for John. Before Jake speeds off in hot pursuit, he asks some of the townspeople to contact the military and inform them of the situation.

Ω

The military is looking for John or confirmation of his death. Between securing the borders, hunting down clones, and feeding the starving public, they have their hands full. But they are accomplishing what John could not with the mess that he created. The military does make contact with the town and learns of John's status, as well as Jake being hot on his trail. They immediately dispatch a small team of soldiers to find and join Jake. That is all of the assistance that the military can spare at the time, but at least Jake will have a military radio. Communication will greatly help Jake.

Ω

In the ridges and hollows of the mountains, there are so many back roads that it would be pure luck if any of the men are traveling the same road as John. If John is truly heading for Eden, they will all end up in the same place. Jake worries about Eden being a decoy and John doubling back and losing them. Frankly, Jake cannot figure out why John would surround himself with the enemy instead of trying to get out of the country, or at least hide somewhere unexpected. The men slow their pursuit and begin stopping to ask more people if they have seen John or the van. Nobody has seen John. The more Jake thinks about it, the more convinced he becomes that they are not on the right track. Jake is beside himself and stressing out trying to figure out where and what John is doing. He has been fretting about what to do for the last thirty miles, until he rolls into the next town and sees a large commotion at a small grocery store.

Ω

John has been physically and emotionally breaking down from stress for a while. Now, hunger is starting to consume him. He could have been in Eden by the next day, but he stopped at the grocery store and seized it by force with his two clones. John and the clones were stuffing their faces with anything that they could get a hold of. The county sheriff, one that John had overlooked with the bacteria, and a pickup load of deputized locals came busting through the doors. A fierce gunfight broke out, and the whole store was completely shredded by bullets. Smoke and floating debris filled the store as the locals bravely exchanged bullets with the clones. The clones killed all but two locals before they got out the door. The sheriff managed to take out one of the clones in the parking lot and riddled the van with bullet holes. The whole town is encircled around the dead clone like it was an alien that dropped out of the sky. They all wanted a good look at the mutant soldier they have heard so much about. Jake is amazed by the local's disregard for their fallen deputies. The town is beaming with pride that they killed a clone and run John off when he came to their town.

Jake and the men quickly take after John. The van does not make it very far before the sheriff's bullets take their toll. John and the clone immediately hijack a car and are on their way within minutes. Jake finds the van and does not know if John is in a nearby house, on foot, or what to expect. The men have to treat the whole area as if John is nearby laying in wait for an ambush. By the time the men secure the area and find out the description of the stolen car, John has put even more distance between them. The military soldiers catch up to Jake before he leaves the van. Jake and the men are awfully glad to see the soldiers rolling in with the flag flying high above their vehicle. The soldiers confirm that the military has taken back the country. The bad news is that the military is depending on Jake and the men to capture John.

The men are all eagerly chasing after John, but the fact that the military is depending on them to capture John puts all of the unwanted pressure back on them. Most of Jake's men assumed that they were about to go home, alive, when they saw the soldiers coming. The see-saw of emotions is starting to wear down Jake's men. Every time the men cheat death, they find it harder to engage in the next skirmish. Every day the odds are tipping out of John's favor and into the men's. Knowing that raises the men's spirits considerably, but everybody is afraid of what John has in store for them at Eden. At every stop the locals have a better idea of exactly where Eden is located. The farther the men go, the closer they can pin point Eden. It's an all out race for Eden now. Jake knows that if he can catch John before he gets there, the men will have a much better chance of succeeding and surviving their mission.

Ω

John has eaten enough at the grocery store to keep his body functional, but within hours his stomach is empty. He feels like he is starving to death all over again. John is very tired and very hungry. It's almost as if he is drunk. He keeps thinking about just making it home, hitting the kitchen, and crawling into his own bed. He tries not to think about how long of a drive he has ahead of him. He just keeps imagining rolling into Eden and all of the stress that he is experiencing will vanish forever. John seems to have the mentality of a teenager who has just got into trouble and running for the safety of home. While John daydreams about home, he keeps slowing down. Jake constantly keeps the hammer down and is slowly closing the gap.

John rolls into a small village that appears to be a ghost town, other than a few cars and other signs of life here and there. It's clear that nothing is going on in this town. But it feels safe, almost like home. John starts to have delusional thoughts about staying in the town and abandoning Eden. He feels some strange emotional yearning for this place, which he does not understand. John pulls into the last house and knocks on the door. A pleasant, older lady answers the door. They lock eyes and John is rendered speechless.

After all these years, John can feel in his heart that he has finally found his family. Tears start to well up in his eyes. He just wants to run inside. Before he can say a word, the woman slowly turns away and gently closes the door in his face. John just stands on the porch, heartbroken. He catches something out of the corner of his eye. People are coming out of their homes with rifles and slowly walking up the street towards him. With tears flowing down his check, John frantically pounds on the door. He looks back down the street, and the small mob is getting closer. He desperately pounds on the door even harder, while begging to be left in. A gunshot rings out. John leaps off the porch and races away.

John blindly races down the road, sobbing uncontrollably as night falls across the forest surrounding him. Hours later, his preoccupied mind realizes that he is hopelessly lost. John and the clone have seen nothing but trees for miles, and neither one of them have a clue where they are. John aimlessly continues to drive through the woods for much of the night. He is completely whipped and pulls the car over. John blankly stares through the windshield and into the night. Right now, he wishes that he had a council bossing him around. If he only knew then what he knows now, his life could have been happy and fulfilling. Finding what he has longed for his entire life but not being able to grasp it is the harshest pill John ever had to swallow. John asks the night sky why he couldn't have found his grandmother sooner. He thinks about the people running him out of his hometown, and his infinite sadness turns to anger. John is come over by a strange feeling of déjà vu.

Both John and the clone sit there silently and motionless, not knowing what to do. John sees a distant light through the trees and drives toward it. The clone can't see the light and grasps the door handle, thinking that John has gone insane. Out of nowhere, a large, stone archway and an iron gate appear in the headlights. As they pass through the gate, John clinches his grip on the steering wheel as the clone clinches its' rifle. Cold chills run down both of their spines. They can feel evil consuming the inside of the car like smoke seeping in through the vents.

John rolls to a stop in front of a massive stone building. He struggles to see where he is in the headlights. John slowly enters through the front doors. He follows the light that is now deep inside the building. The clone reluctantly follows with its rifle to its shoulder. Once inside, John knows he has been here before. As he cautiously walks down the large corridor, he realizes that this is where he was born. The light stops moving away from John. He creeps closer and can see that the light is a young woman. John slowly continues until he stands face to face with the woman. She is a beautiful sight and covered with a long white shroud. She smiles at John, conveying her unconditional love. John is awestruck. It has to be his mother. John holds out his arms to hug his mother. A creepy, evil man appears out of the wall and stands beside her, laughing at John the whole time. John steps back in shock. The man rips off the shroud covering Lucy's body and laughs even harder. John gasps for breath when he sees his beloved mother's naked body with a giant, red, bony hand with thick black claws, clinching her from behind. The demon's thumb and three fingers wrap around Lucy's ribs with its claws gently piercing into her belly. The index finger lay up over her shoulder and pierces into her chest. Small drops of blood trickle down Lucy's body from the claws. John watches his mother's smiling face turn to anguish. John screams and chases the man down the hall, with the creep laughing the whole way.

Ω

The asylum is a maze of rooms and corridors. John quickly looses track of the man and his way. With every turn that John makes, there is another hallucination of people harming him or his mother. John has no idea who these people are, or why they are doing these things. Every one of them has the same demon hand around them. It's like children playing with dolls. The asylum is showing John his heritage and making him understand, although he is denying everything. Eventually, John enters a room and there is the evil man raping his mother. John instantly runs from the room. He refuses the knowledge that the pure evil man is his father. John frantically searches for a way out of the asylum. Everywhere he turns, there is the man raping his mother, over and over, looking at John and laughing every time. Eventually John finds his way to the entrance. There is the evil man just standing there laughing at John on the other side of a window. John stares through the glass at the man and can see the demon hand slowly crawling up the man's back like a spider. John intensely watches as the man's face begins to change. John realizes that he is looking at his own reflection in the glass. As he watches the hand start to close around his image, he feels the pressure enclosing his body. John freaks and burst out the door on a dead sprint for the car. John peels out of the asylum and never looks back.

Ω

It's breaking daylight, and eventually John gets his bearings and heads for Eden. He is concentrating so intensely on convincing himself that his visions are not true, he doesn't realize that he has left behind his only protection and weapon. John has nothing to do but run now. He disengages his mind and drives down the road like a lifeless machine. Eden is only hours away, and John's not stopping for nothing. He finally rolls into Eden late in the afternoon. He has beaten his enemies to his stronghold. He is eager to see some friendly faces, but nobody is out and about. John is intrigued but thinks nothing more about it.

He heads straight for the mess hall. John busts through the doors like a kid on Christmas morning and runs straight to the kitchen. There is nobody there either, but more importantly, there is no food. John frantically searches every cupboard and every cooler for anything at all to eat. Eventually, he stops looking and stands in the middle of the kitchen trembling. John can't understand what is going on. He starts running from house to house and building to building looking for his family. There is not one person there. Eden is a ghost town.

As John staggers through the middle of town, he wonders if the military has already been there. He starts running for the clone lab and the underground barracks. John lets out a sigh of relief when he finds two clone units underground. As he walks around, he notices that the barracks and labs are in shambles. The only people there are the terrorist and a handful of lab assistants. Nobody says a word, and John can feel in the pit of his stomach that something has gone horribly wrong. He runs for the President's cell. It's empty. John slowly walks back and asks the terrorist what the hell has happened. The terrorist explains to John that his followers gathered up all the children and left, taking all the food and money that they could find. Shortly after that, Dr. Janzen sprung the president and they both escaped. The rest were starving and slowly left a few at a time. Even most of the young women and their clones that spread the bacteria had left.

Ω

John just stands there staring at the wall and not making a sound. In his head he is screaming and yelling at everybody for losing control of his operation. He is also fantasizing about killing everybody who has abandoned him. After a while, John comes to his senses and realizes that he has been staring at some food on the table. The clones are not being trained to fight because they are too busy scrounging around the local area for food. When they find some scraps, they bring them back to the barracks and share them with the terrorist and his assistants. John starts stuffing the food into his head by the fistfuls. After he is full, he finds the closest bed and simply goes to sleep.

Ω

Jake, his men, and the soldiers find Eden just before dark. They decide to wait until morning to make a move. They take shifts staking out the town while the others sleep.

Ω

John wakes about an hour before daylight. He lay in the dark, trying to decide if his memories are a dream or real. John is desperately hoping that it is all a bad dream. Reality sets in, and John sits on the edge of the bed sobbing. Never before has he felt so betrayed and helpless. John staggers to the lab looking for more food, but it is all gone. The terrorist runs in and starts frantically yelling at John that Eden is under attack. Jake and the men are moving in and searching through every building. John just sits in a chair and stares at the ceiling in a comatose state. The terrorist takes control and orders the clones out to fight Jake.

The clones swarm out of the ground like yellow jackets and charge the men while showering them with bullets. The men duck and dive for cover, but a few are already gunned down. Eden is basically a wide blacktop road with a row of buildings down both sides. The only cover is between the buildings. Both the men and the clones are tucked in between the buildings and shooting around the corners at each other. Jake wants to fall back to the creek bed and call in an air strike, but the men are trapped. The men start busting out windows and kicking in doors to retreat through the buildings instead of around them. The clones do not even know that the men are getting away from them.

Eventually, the clones realize that nobody is shooting back at them. The clones charge up along the side of the buildings, only to find out that there is nobody around the corners. By the time the clones finally figure out what is going on and run to the end of the buildings, most of the men have already made it into the creek bed. There are a few stragglers still running through the field towards the creek. A hand-ful of clones sprint from the edge of town and begin to chase them down. The clones are about half way to the creek when the last straggler dives down over the creek bank. As the last man disappears into the creek, the rest of the men pop their heads up over the bank like gophers and open fire on the rushing clones. The clones about break their necks trying to get turned around and back to the buildings for cover, but none of them make it.

The clones and the men are exchanging heavy fire again. The men have good cover but still have nowhere to go but up and down the creek bed. Jake gives the nod to the soldier to call in the coordinates of Eden and green light an air strike. It's not long until the clones hear the screaming of the jets as they bear down on Eden. The clones start running for their lives as buildings start blowing up all around them. Clones are scattering in every direction. The ones that are pinned down between the buildings have to take cover flat on their faces in the middle of the road, including the terrorist. Somehow the fire and force of the blasts go right over top of the clones and the terrorist, and they all survive.

When Jake sees the clones fleeing through the fields, he orders the men to completely surround Eden and shoot anything that comes running out. As near as Jake can tell, what is left of John's entire army is trapped inside of Eden. He does not want any loose ends. A bomb hits John's warehouse where he has been hoarding the fuel reserves. The explosion shakes the ground under everybody's feet. Everything comes to a halt while they all watch the giant mushroom cloud roll into the air. Everything is burning now, including the underground bunkers. The fire forces John and the others to the surface. John stands in the middle of Eden, at the spot where he had planned to be the courtyard of his palace. He slowly spins, looking at everything that is burning all around him. He has a pistol and puts it to his head, but John is much to full of himself to pull the trigger.

The surviving clones are sneaking up along the side of the destroyed buildings and heading for the woods behind Eden. The terrorist jumps out from behind a corner and in front of the clones. He begins yelling and screaming at the clones to turn around and fight. He gets right in the leading clone's face, calls it a coward and tells it that if it does not fight, it will be executed. The clone raises both arms high in the air and smashes both fists down on top of the terrorist's shoulders. The terrorist's whole body compresses about five inches, flinging him backwards. He lands sitting up against an underground utility box. As the terrorist sits against the box, his wits slowly start coming back to him. He looks for the clones, but they are long gone. He starts to realize that both of his shoulders are completely destroyed, and his spine is snapped in two. He cannot move a thing, except his head. An oily sludge from the warehouse is on fire and oozing all over Eden. The burning sludge looks like lava, only thinner and faster moving. The terrorist is sitting up on the curb, and his feet are down on the road. He notices the sludge oozing down the road along the curb. It's heading right for his feet. The terrorist begins to yell for help, but nobody is around. Then he sees John and begs for help. John just cracks a little smile and walks away.

The closer the sludge comes to the terrorist's feet, the more he begins to panic. No matter how hard he tries, he cannot move a muscle. The sludge slowly and relentlessly keeps oozing towards his feet. The terrorist begins to hyperventilate. In an act of shear desperation, he begins to flail his head around like a fish out of water. The sludge surrounds his feet, and they instantly burst into flames. The terrorist leaves out such a loud agonizing scream that everybody stops in their tracks and looks towards the horrific sound. He can't feel a thing in his legs, but it's the absolute terror of watching your own body burn that fuels the agony. When the fire reaches his knees, he starts to beat the back of his head into the utility box, trying to end his life. After about twenty times of smashing his head against the box, he realizes that he can't get enough leverage. His adrenaline is pumping so hard that he can't even dull his senses. The fire is halfway between his knees and hips, and his face starts to blister from the heat. He feels the excruciating pain for the first time through the whole ordeal. He just closes his eyes, turns his face away, and screams until he finally succumbs from the heat and smoke scorching his lungs.

Ω

Jake and the men are busy chasing after clones and taking prisoners as they stumble out of the smoke and fire. John is still blundering around inside of his burning town. Jake catches sight of John, and he moves in for a shot. John appears to be in shock and completely surrounded by fire. John is not in shock. He is thinking about how he can get his neck out of the noose that seems to be tightening by the second. He is looking for a place where he can disappear into the fire and slip away on the other side. Hopefully everybody will think that he is dead. John finds exactly what he is looking for and starts moving towards the gap in the fire.

Jake moves into position and marks John with his crosshairs. Jake is about to end it once and for all when he notices something out of the corner of his eye. It's Nate again. He is running right into the path between Jake's rifle and John. Nate is charging full bore to tackle John. John hears him coming and wheels around with his pistol. Nate quickly grabs the gun out of John's hand and punches him right in the mouth, knocking him to the ground flat on his back. Fire is closing in on the both of them. Nate grabs John by the front of his shirt and jerks him to his feet. Nate stands within inches of John's face and looks deep into his eyes. Nate slowly tells John everything that he holds dear to his heart about his family. He talks about how young and beautiful his wife was, and how she has never ever harmed another living creature her entire life. He goes on to tell John how precious and innocent his two-year-old daughter was. Nate tightly clinches his hands around John's neck, and explains in horrific detail how they both died. It's getting hotter by the second. Nate tightens his grip a little and tells John that they are going to Hell together so he can torture John for all eternity.

Nate actually has a couple of seconds of satisfaction while looking at the fear in John's eyes. The flames are getting closer and higher. There is only one way out of the inferno now, which is where Jake is, and it's closing off fast. Jake yells at Nate to get out of the fire and not to worry because he has John dead to rights. Nate looks at Jake with an expression of satisfaction and peace, as if to say that everything is all right. For all that Nate has been through and as far as he has come, Jake hates to see him die now. Jake yells to Nate and asks him if he thinks that his wife and daughter are watching and waiting for him. Jake yells out, "How do you think they're going to feel if you choose avenging their deaths over getting to see them again? You will be abandoning them."

205

All three men just stand there not moving or saying a thing. Nate leaves out a moaning scream while he rolls his head around. Nate then punches John, knocking him to the ground again. He starts running full bore towards Jake. The gap in the flames has closed, but the flames are not very high yet. Nate hurdles through towards Jake.

Nate rolls to the ground with his pants legs on fire. He and Jake frantically pat them out. When the flames are out, they both jump to their feet to watch John. John is just now struggling back to his feet. He looks around and realizes that there is no escape. He positions himself right in the middle of the road and prays that the fire will not reach him. John nervously prances around as the temperature rises to about two degrees under unbearable. The flames climb higher and higher. They seem to be dancing around John. Jake and Nate begin to see what appears to be a face forming in the wall of fire behind John. A deep, evil voice that seems to be coming from everywhere says, "You have failed me. It's time to come home." John wheels around, looks at the face, and for the first time he understands and accepts his life with tears welling in his eyes. He is not the right hand of God. He is the right hand of Satan himself. The Devil has been manipulating John's life since before he was even born. Satan is John's true father. With a loud roar, the ground caves in under John's feet. Flames shoot out of the hole and high into the sky as John's screams disappear into the ground.

$$\Omega$$

Jake and Nate just look at each other, not knowing what to think. Both of them are scared to death, and they slowly back away from the burning pit. Eventually, the fire dies down and the prisoners are all hauled away. All of the surviving militia attempt to relax, as they cautiously accept the fact that their nightmare is over and they have survived. Jake and Nate eventually walk over to where John fell into the hole and realize that one of John's underground barracks has caved in. They look through the burnt rubble for John's body, but cannot find it. At first they think the sneaky bastard snuck through the underground labyrinth and escaped. Eventually, they decide that no human could have survived the fire. They both wonder if the phenomenon that they had witnessed can be logically explained, or if a logical explanation will hide the phenomenon. Whichever the case may be, neither one of them will ever be the same again.

Ω

The President has already returned to his office and working on the seemingly impossible task of piecing the country back together. He flies to Eden to personally thank each and every man for the sacrifices that they have made and get the names of the ones who had died for their country. Each man is invited to join the military and help with reconstructing the country, which mostly will consist of dealing with refugees. Anyone else can immediately return home and be with their families. The men are all saying good-bye and anxiously heading for their homes. Besides Jake, Nate is the only one who has no family to run to. Jake invites Nate to return to the capital with him. Nate whole-heartedly thanks Jake for looking after him so much and keeping him on the right track. He regretfully declines Jake's offer. Nate needs to go home.

Ω

As soon as the President returns to the capital, he appoints Jake as the new vice president. This is a great honor for Jake, but it will be a very tough job to do over the next few years and he intensely commits to it. Jake soon realizes that dealing with the aftermath of massive death and destruction is much harder than fighting John. The thing that Jake worries the most about in the future is somebody picking up where John left off. Jake lobbies to keep the burnt rubble of Eden exactly the way it is. He has a monument for John placed at the edge of the hole where he fell to his death. Jake wants it to be a physical reminder for future generations not to get too full of themselves.

Ω

Nate makes the long, painful journey home. He walks down his lane and catches sight of his house. He falls to his knees and with tears in his eyes, he begs God to leave him see his wife and daughter in the yard. Nate knows that his family is gone, but he never really did get any confirmation. He knew it was foolish to keep an ember of hope burning in his heart, but it helped maintain his will to live. And after what he has just witnessed, anything is possible. There is not even a moving insect to be seen, and eventually Nate gets up off of his knees and continues walking towards the house. It's as if he is walking through a tunnel that leads right to where he has last seen his wife alive. He rounds the corner of the house and sees her still lying there naked in the grass. Nate runs to her side and stands there hopelessly starring at her laying on her back with her hands crossed over her chest as if she were laying in a coffin. She looks so peaceful and beautiful. Nate falls to his knees and bursts into tears. He cradles her in his arms and tries to wake her up. But her body is cold and stiff.

Ω

Nate holds his dead wife for hours until he can cry no more. As the reality of his loss sets in, he gently lays his wife down and begins to look around. Nate is looking at all of the dead clones in his yard. He notices that the coyotes and buzzards have been eating at them, but his wife is untouched. He gathers her up and takes her to a rolling hill that overlooks the farm. In the past, when one of them would get depressed or stressed out, the whole family would picnic on the hill. They would look down on their home and remind themselves to appreciate each other and be grateful for what they had. Nate digs a grave in the best spot on the hill and buries his wife. He returns to the house at dark and starts burning the rotting clone bodies in their own fire pit.

Ω

Early in the following morning, Nate hikes up the mountain to look for his daughter's body. As he walks through the woods, he keeps thinking about what his daughter must have gone through. He figures that she was probably confused and wondering why her daddy was not protecting her like he always has before. Nate cannot help but to feel like he left his wife and daughter down. He searches all day and does not find one trace of his daughter. He returns home that night, and his daughter's cat is waiting at the door. Nate gets angry when he sees the cat and is about to kick it off of the porch, when something stops him in his tracks. He knows that the cat means the world to his daughter. He thinks about how upset she would be if he hurt her cat. Nate looks straight into the night sky and promises his little girl that he will take good care of her cat.

Ω

Nate searches the mountain all weekend, every weekend, looking for a sign of his daughter, but never finds anything. He is depressed and very lonely. After a while he starts to talk to the cat as if it is his daughter. Nate eats, sleeps, and plays with the cat just like he did with his daughter. Eventually, the cat dies. Nate buries it beside his wife and marks the grave with his daughter's name. He digs a grave for himself and leaves instructions with a local friend that he is to be buried there also. The only thing that Nate has to look forwards to is dying. He is going to stay strong and live right to ensure that he will see his family again. Every night before he goes to sleep, he prays to God to bring him home. Every morning when he wakes up, is another day of heartache. Nate has a feeling that he is going to live to be ninety and knows that he has a long, miserable life ahead of him.

Ω

What is left of John's former congregation has spread out across the country to open up orphanages for the children who had everything taken from them. They are a significant help in feeding and sheltering the homeless refugees also. Dr. Janzen was imprisoned for his role in the deaths of millions of innocent citizens. He is released on parole, in care of the congregation, in order to help people rebuild their lives. His release is a reward for freeing the President. The President also knows that the constant visual of the result of his actions will be a worse punishment than sitting in a prison cell. It's hard on Dr. Janzen. Eventually, it gets to the point where he can't take it anymore, and he shoots himself in the head.

Ω

Lucky Jim returns home to his family and is living the good life, until he surprises an armed robber late one night at a convenience store. Jim is shot through the heart and dies instantly. The shooter is later apprehended, and it is discovered that she is one of John's clones who helped spread the bacteria. She was struggling to survive in the world all alone. The news spreads like wildfire and starts a nationwide panic. Nobody knows for sure how many of John's brain-washed followers and their clones are out there, or what they will do. Identical twins have to go into hiding. Innocent twins are gunned down across the country for fear that they are clones. Many stories circulate around that there are still clone soldiers hiding in the mountains and swamps, and even in the city ruins. Eden is placed under a twenty-four hour a-day surveillance in case any stragglers show up.

Ω

A year flies by and not one person ever sets foot inside of Eden again. The surveillance is eventually lifted, and the people's fears subside a little. Jake finally has some time to spare and decides that he is going to visit Eden. As Jake strolls through Eden, a flood of emotions is pouring into his head and chest. Although he has spent every day for the past year rebuilding what John has destroyed, he quickly realizes that he has suppressed many bad memories. Jake feels the need to relieve the emotional pressure in his heart, but he does not know if he is angry or sad or even who's fault it all is. Then in a flash, it all disappears when he catches movement out of the corner of his eye. It's a young boy and a toddler playing in a pile of dirt. Then Jake notices a woman standing in front of John's monument. Jake's mind races with possibilities of who these people are and what they are doing there. He cautiously approaches them, not sure what to expect. Jake stands behind the woman and gently clears his throat. He frightens her, and she quickly wheels around to face Jake. It's Amy.

Ω

Jake has no idea who Amy is, and he apologizes for scaring her. As he nervously fidgets around, he tries to politely ask Amy who she is and if she knew John. Amy introduces herself and tells Jake that she has known John since grade school. She then adds that no matter what he has done, she will always be grateful to him. He helped her out of a bad relationship and helped piece her life together, which lead to meeting her wonderful husband. Amy then bluntly tells Jake that she knew John before all of this. Jake relaxes and continues a short conversation with Amy until she tells him that she has to go.

Jake watches Amy walk away and call her kids. The older boy goes to her right away, but the toddler ignores her and keeps playing in the dirt. Jake chuckles and turns around to look down into the hole where John fell. He faintly hears Amy say in a soft but scalding tone, "John come on." Jake wheels back around with a look of fear in his eyes.

The boy jumps up from the dirt, runs to the middle of the road and stares at Jake with his beady little eyes. He gives Jake a big devilish grin and runs to his mother.

Meet Author Michael T. Henry

Mike Henry can be found aimlessly roaming the ridges and hollows, somewhere in Fulton County PA, searching through his heart that belongs to an earlier time. A chronic thinker with a debilitating imagination, he struggles to find his place in modern society. He is amazed how mankind's logical oblivion hides the secrets that whisper past everybody's ears. Mike's suppressed mind has escaped from under the thumb of conformity, and his throbbing brain is seeping through his fingers and onto paper. Writing is a welcome release in which he is addicted to. Mike is very anxious, maybe even a little frightened of where his mind will take him. He's definitely willing for you to read all about it.